A Better Tomorrow

by
Charles Rammelkamp

AmErica House
Baltimore

© 2001 by Charles Rammelkamp.
All rights reserved. No part of this book may be reproduced in any form without written permission from the publishers, except by a reviewer who may quote brief passages in a review to be printed in a newspaper or magazine.

First printing

ISBN: 1-59129-023-6
PUBLISHED BY AMERICA HOUSE BOOK PUBLISHERS
www.publishamerica.com
Baltimore

Printed in the United States of America

This book is dedicated to Abby, without whom none of this could ever have been imagined.

Acknowledgments

"A Diaspora of the Mind" originally appeared in *The Midday Moon*. "The Unkindest Cut," "The Tenth Man" and "A Hint of Figs" have appeared in or been accepted by *The Small Pond of Literature*. "The Hebrew Lesson," "Hair and Share," "No, He's the Dumb One" and "Family Secrets" all appeared in *Princeton Arts Review* as "Kleinpoppen Chronicles." "The Ultimate Checkmate," "Redemption" and "The Shikker Rabbi" all appeared in the online venue *New Works Review*. "Just Say Yes" was in *Heliotrope*. "Rosencrantz and Guildenstern Are Jews" appeared in *Happy*. "Guard My Tongue" has been accepted for publication in *The Iconoclast*, and "God Is Everything, Mostly" has been accepted for publication in the online venue, *EWGPresents*.

Table of Contents

A Diaspora of the Mind..9

The Unkindest Cut..19

The Hebrew Lesson..27

Hair and Share...33

No, He's the Dumb One...35

Family Secrets..37

The Ultimate Checkmate..43

Valhalla...51

Redemption...63

Mishpocheh...73

One in Every Generation..79

The Shikker Rabbi..89

Just Say Yes..101

The Tenth Man..109

God Is Everything, Mostly...115

Guard My Tongue..125

Rosencrantz and Guildenstern Are Jews..................................135

A Hint of Figs..141

A Diaspora of the Mind

"There were seven Jewish families in Potawatomi Rapids when I was growing up," Robert Kleinpoppen told his children. "The Hirsches, the Shapiros, the Gottliebs, the Goldbergs, the Rosenblooms—oh, gosh, I can't remember who they all were now, it's been twenty-five, thirty years. But there were seven families, that much I'm sure of. I think there were enough men for a minyan, but there wasn't a synagogue in town. They had to go to Kalamazoo to attend a synagogue."

"You weren't Jewish then, were you, Daddy?" His eight-year old daughter Leah's question sounded almost like an accusation. Kleinpoppen knew she did not consider him as "authentically" Jewish as she did her mother; he'd converted a dozen years earlier when he married Judy; but was he being paranoid about his daughter?

"No. I was still nominally a Christian, though we didn't go to church." Was he defending himself?

"Daddy's a Jew," Judy told their daughter. "He's just as Jewish as you and I are." She was likewise aware of their daughter's doubts; she wondered if it came about from the Jewish day school she and her brother attended, from her classmates and their parents' pedigrees.

Kleinpoppen recalled that his parents-in-law had been dubious about his conversion. But then, he'd only met them after he'd already begun the process, presented to Judy's parents as a *fait accompli*, since they had strong objections to her marrying outside the faith. But they seemed to accept him now, he thought, at least as much as they accepted either of their sons-in-law or their daughter-in-law in to the family circle, and Marty and Mandy had both been born Jewish.

"Why not?" Leah asked her father.

"Why didn't we go to church? Nobody went to church in the God-Is-Dead sixties."

"What?" Leah looked puzzled. *God Is Dead?*

"We didn't go to church. My father didn't make us. He didn't go and he didn't see why my brothers and I should have to, either. So we didn't. We slept late and watched cartoons on Sunday mornings like everybody else."

"Did you know any of the Jews?"

"As a matter of fact, Mike Shapiro and I hung around together for several years. We were the same age, in the same class. He went away to private school in Connecticut after the ninth grade, and our friendship faded; we drifted apart."

"Oh yeah," Judy said. "Mike Shapiro."

"His father ran for mayor of Potawatomi Rapids. Vic Shapiro. He ran against this Polish guy named Joe Buinowski, one of those Lech Walesa-looking heavyset guys with thick hair and a granite jaw. His sister Joanne ran the only record store in town, Moore's Music Shop. She was married to Donald Moore, a guy I never met.

"But once, Mike and I went into her record store to look at the latest rock and roll offerings. We were teenagers, and the Rolling Stones and the Beatles and the Animals and all those British rock groups were just becoming popular. Anyway, so we walked into the store, and Joanne, who was this really imposing looking woman, like a hippo or a rhino, a big warty thick-skinned animal of some sort—she had big brown warts all over her neck, I remember, and on the backs of her hands. Anyway, she reared back and bellowed at Mike, 'You get out of here before I spill your kike blood all over the street!'"

"Did she really?"

"I don't know what prompted it other than sisterly affection. I mean, as far as I knew, Vic and Joe weren't hostile toward each other. But it was pretty sad."

"I'd say so."

"I've never told you this before?"

"I've heard you talk about Mike Shapiro, at least I think I have, but I'd never heard that story."

"Did I tell you how the fourth grade teacher used to put him on the spot every morning when we recited the Lord's Prayer?"

"Yes," Judy said, remembering. "That's how I remember the name."

"Every morning we'd recite the Pledge of Allegiance and the Lord's Prayer," Robert said for his daughter's benefit, even though she wasn't paying attention any longer. "When we got to the Lord's Prayer, Miss Wolfe would announce, 'Mike doesn't have to recite this because he's Jewish and he doesn't believe in God.' She sounded so gleeful saying it, and she said it every single morning, in case we'd forgotten overnight."

"Doesn't believe in God! Didn't he challenge her?"

"We were only in fourth grade."

"What does he do these days?"

"Mike? He fled that place as quick as he could. Prep school, Columbia, and now he's down in South America working for Amnesty International. Talk about a diaspora. If America is a diaspora within a diaspora, Mike's destiny always seemed to me a diaspora *within* a diaspora within a diaspora. Alienation cubed."

"And you?"

"Me?"

"What do you attribute your alienation to?"

"You think I'm alienated?" The thought had never really occurred to him, and he didn't have an answer. He turned to his daughter instead. "Okay, Leah, get your shoes on while I hunt down your brother and let's get going to the babysitter's."

* * *

"You're in early today, Bob." George Romanchuck, the project manager, watched Kleinpoppen sign in. Kleinpoppen was a technical writer on a government software support contract. His consulting firm occupied a row of cubicles on the fifth floor of a ten-story federal office building.

"My kids're off school today, so I got to drop them off at the sitter's and leave a little earlier than usual."

"School's not out this early, is it? It's only the fifth of June."

"No, they just have the day off from school. It's Shavuot."

"What's Shav-oo-whatever-you-said?" Romanchuck was a Polish guy from Detroit who affected a good old boy Southern drawl. A man in his mid-fifties, Romanchuck had lived in Virginia for about twenty years.

"Jewish holiday. It comes 50 days after the second day of Passover. It marks Moses receiving the Ten Commandments on Mount Sinai. Seven weeks times seven days plus one."

"Boy, you guys take off a day for everything."

"The Christians have a similar holiday, 50 days after Easter. Pentecost. I'm not sure what it stands for. The Holy Ghost doing something or other. But they basically ripped it off from the Jews. The mystical number seven squared, you know."

"The Jews probably got it from the Catholics." Romanchuck sounded a little defensive, but Kleinpoppen didn't really take it seriously. He was feeling chatty.

"No, the Jews came before the Catholics. That's just history. That's a fact."

"You aren't a Jew."

"Sure I am. I converted."

"But you weren't born a Jew."

"No, but I converted."

"I'm as Jewish as you are, Bob."

Kleinpoppen laughed and shook his head in mock disbelief. Of course he knew what Romanchuck was getting at. The Jew as some other sort of species. It was amazing, all the stereotypes of Jews, often contradictory. Either they were left-wing communist revolutionaries or right-wing oppressors of Palestinians. Greedy bastards or ultra-idealists. "It's a religion,

George."

Romanchuck looked skeptical. "What did you do to convert? You have to study a lot of stuff?"

"Basically it's the conversion ceremony that makes the difference, but I did take a crash course in Judaism."

"What, did you have to learn Hebrew and all that?"

"A little, just to get by in services. Twenty-two weeks of study, the Jewish calendar, the holidays, the rituals." Kleinpoppen gestured vaguely. "But it was the conversion ceremony that was the central thing, and that's an immersion, like a Baptism. Another thing the Christians ripped off from the Jews." Kleinpoppen could see this annoyed Romanchuck, and he needled him a little more. "Oh, and of course, you have to be circumcised."

Romanchuck looked horrified. "You mean, they cut off your dick?"

Kleinpoppen laughed. "I was already circumcised, but I did have to go through a 'token' circumcision, which was a little weird. I mean, circumcision is circumcision, but as the sign of the covenant with Abraham, you have to go through a ritual. So they sprayed a local anesthetic on one of the less sensitive areas of my penis and the mohel lanced it, drew blood, while the other rabbis mumbled prayers. It was kind of weird. But if I *hadn't* been circumcised previously, I would have had to get one."

"I'm not circumcised," Romanchuck said. "No way I'm going to convert to Judaism."

Kleinpoppen laughed. "Well, let me know if you change your mind. I can recommend a mohel."

"Not me, no way!"

"I'm going to go down for some coffee." Kleinpoppen turned away from Romanchuck's office and headed for the elevators.

* * *

Kleinpoppen stood on the square brown tiles of the cafeteria contemplating the morning fare. Fluorescent lights in the high ceiling glared off the polished stainless steel compartments containing sausages, pancakes and scrambled eggs, shielded by slanting plate glass windows, as in a display case. Fat black women in white uniforms, with spatulas and forks in their hands, stood behind the displays, waiting to take orders. Kleinpoppen poured a cup of coffee from the huge steel urn into a styrofoam cup and plucked a cellophane-wrapped bagel from a tray and stood in line to pay the blind cashier. His turn came at last.

"Bagel and a cup of coffee, Joe."

"Morning, Bob," Joe said. He perched on a high stool over the cash register, his blank face staring ahead of him. He punched some keys on his talking cash register. "One dollar and thirty-seven cents," the robot voice said.

"Thanks." Kleinpoppen collected his change and his breakfast and headed for the door.

"You say I can get a*head* if I open a retirement account? I'd sure like some *head*."

Kleinpoppen turned to see Ev Baker behind him, making his usual sexually suggestive conversation with a woman. Baker was another guy on the contract. He was big, like an overgrown farmboy. He seemed to wear his gut like a badge; Kleinpoppen always got the impression Baker looked to his weight for a sense of authority. Bantering like the buffoon he was with his puerile jokes, Baker sounded like a high school kid to Kleinpoppen; to himself, Baker sounded witty, clever, a veritable late night television talkshow host. Baker was a pal of Romanchuck's. Somehow he'd helped Romanchuck's company win the software contract.

Kleinpoppen left the cafeteria and headed back to the elevators.

* * *

14

Baker and Romanchuck were walking ahead of Kleinpoppen to the elevators. They were all going to the same weekly status meeting. Baker was talking in a low voice. Kleinpoppen caught a few words, enough to get the gist. Baker was describing a sexual fantasy involving a woman who worked in another division. Romanchuck seemed amused. It was a rather brutal fantasy, involving yanked-apart legs, blood and screaming. Baker turned around and caught sight of Kleinpoppen.

"I was just telling George what I'd like to do to Karen Delancey."

"So I heard."

"Hey, Kleinpoppen. George said you were telling him about getting a 'token circumcision' when you converted to Judaism." He laughed. "What'd they do, stick pins in your dick?" He laughed again, a loud, bantering bray.

Kleinpoppen felt he'd been betrayed by Romanchuck, but immediately reflected that he hadn't spoken to him about it in confidence. Besides, Baker was Romanchuck's confidante if anybody was. Still, Kleinpoppen regretted having spoken freely about the details of his conversion. He wondered what line Romanchuck had taken when he told Baker.

"Ouch! Oh!" Baker grabbed his crotch in a kind of slapstick comedy routine, and he and Romanchuck howled. It seemed to Kleinpoppen that they were laughing at him. The poor sucker who converted to Judaism. "Man, that is so freaky, what those Jews do. You let them do it to you, too, huh?"

"Hey, I've got a lawsuit pending. Can't talk about it." Kleinpoppen hoped this would shut him up, but Baker kept it up all the way to the conference room, grabbing his crotch and talking about getting stuck, laughing at his own jokes.

* * *

At three o'clock, Baker and Romanchuck came down the

aisle to sign out for the day. The two were thick as thieves. As he passed Kleinpoppen's cubicle, his voice saturated with comic irony, Baker said, "How's it hangin'?"

Kleinpoppen knew what was coming. "Pretty low."

"Low and outside," Romanchuck said. He was signing out, too. He and Baker were leaving together.

"How's it hangin'?" Baker repeated. "Got pins and tacks in it?" He laughed at his witty remarks.

"You ought to know. You've sucked it enough," Kleinpoppen returned. He couldn't keep the impatience out of his voice. Romanchuck looked at him, cross.

"Better watch it."

"See you guys tomorrow," Kleinpoppen said, conceding nothing. He heard their voices receding down the hallway toward the elevators.

* * *

"Unfortunately, I told Romanchuck about my token circumcision this morning," Kleinpoppen mentioned to his wife that night as they got ready for bed. "He told Ev Baker about it, and Baker made it into this big joke."

"Oh, Jesus," Judy commiserated. She understood what must have happened.

"Yeah, it just came up somehow. It was Shavuot, and Andy and Leah were off school, and he asked me why I was in early. One thing led to another and I told him about it. He must have gone over to Baker's cube and blabbed about it. I wonder how he put it."

"So then Baker ridiculed you."

"I should have known Romanchuck would tell him."

"Are you ashamed?"

"I don't like having my genitals in the public domain, for one thing. Also, I didn't appreciate Baker's tone, as if he had something on me. You know?"

"Do you think they would have said it to me?"

"Because you were born Jewish?"

"Yes. Or to Mike Shapiro? Do you think they thought it was okay to tease you because they don't really see you as a Jew? Maybe they were just teasing you as though you were really one of them. You know, 'good-natured fun.' Including you as one of the good old boys."

It was something Kleinpoppen had not even considered, and it struck him with the force of self-discovery. Maybe they *were* including him in their laughter at the Jews. And if they were, what should he make of that?

"Maybe," he said to Judy, and he wondered again all at once about the nature of his own alienation. Why *did* he feel apart from the people he worked with? Pogroms of the spirit; a diaspora of the mind.

The Unkindest Cut

"You know, I just hope Andy doesn't wind up with one of those trademark weak chins of the Jaffes," Judy Kleinpoppen said to her mother on the day of her newborn son's bris milah. She held the baby in her arms, looking at him fondly, speculatively, as if to divine what the future held in store for him. She did not say this with any passionate conviction. Possibly, her remark only meant that in her heart she believed her child was probably fated to have a receding chin the way some boys are genetically predestined to baldness or nearsightedness, but Marilyn Felser took the remark as a stinging insult about her stock; her father, his brothers and sisters, Marilyn and her brothers and sisters all had weak chins; they were not so unattractive in the females, who had a kind of big-eyed birdlike prettiness that the retreating lower jaw accentuated, but the men all had to wear beards in order to escape looking like some sort of half-formed sea creatures. Indeed, they all looked handsome and distinguished in beards, but still, they had no choice *but* to wear beards.

Marilyn, never shy about speaking her mind, reacted like a cat whose tail has been stepped upon. The Jaffe weak chin had always been a secret source of anguish. "Well I just hope to God he doesn't wind up looking like a Nazi like your husband's family, with those square chins and the little putty dab noses. The cruel Stormtrooper blue eyes."

Robert Kleinpoppen had just walked into the living room of the Kleinpoppen's Baltimore rowhouse when his mother-in-law made her rather vicious observations. Hurt even more than Marilyn for having simply walked into what sounded like a gratuitous slight, he retreated into the hallway so that neither woman knew he had heard.

"I even had my doubts that you'd have Andy circumcised, if you want to know the truth," Marilyn went on.

"Well I don't want to know. Besides, Robert converted. He didn't have to, but he did."

"But he still gave Andy that middle name." To Kleinpoppen's ears, it sounded like his mother-in-law had stored up a whole catalog of misgivings, suspicions and regrets about her son-in-law. He'd insisted on the middle name of Michael, after his father. The trouble was, Robert's father was still alive, and the Ashkenazi custom was to name children after deceased relatives. Out in the hallway, Kleinpoppen spotted the silver dagger letter opener on the desk by the front door and briefly contemplated cutting out Marilyn Felser's tongue. Let her find another way to insult somebody. Then the doorbell rang and he made noises as if he had just entered the hallway to receive the guests, and Marilyn and Judy, still cradling Andrew, also came out to greet their company.

* * *

The guests started drifting in around two o'clock that clear October afternoon. Not that there were many; it was Wednesday, after all, the eighth day after Andrew's birth, an awkward time for most people to get off work or to come in from out of town. Even though a dairy luncheon was being catered by a local kosher deli for the occasion, it wasn't exactly a party, this ancient welcoming rite. Mainly Judy's family came; many of them also lived in Baltimore—her brother, Ben and his family, the Felser grandparents, a couple of cousins. A nephew, Michael, an undergraduate at Johns Hopkins, was also invited, and several of Judy's friends from work. Kleinpoppen had not invited anybody himself, though he had briefly considered inviting Alice Kilgallen, a woman from work with whom he was involved on a naming standards project. But when he'd talked about the circumcision with Alice, she had said some things that had angered him, and he didn't.

"What a barbaric practice!" she said almost at once, with the vehemence of a right-to-lifer condemning abortion. "Are you really going to subject your son to *that*?"

Alice Kilgallen had been raised a Baptist, though both she and her lapsed Irish Catholic husband, Joe, professed to be atheists. Alice had majored in Anthropology at Kent State, which was one of the reasons Kleinpoppen had thought she might be interested in coming.

"Oh, come on, Alice. Lighten up. He's not going to feel it, particularly. He certainly won't remember it."

"There's evidence now that babies *do* feel the pain, quite specifically. It's a question of medical ethics, circumcision."

"There's no lasting trauma as far as I can tell. People have been circumcised for several millennia now."

"The world is hardly an idyllic place."

"You aren't blaming that on circumcision, are you?"

"Some child psychologists have done studies that suggest permanent psychological scarring."

"Well, at least it's easier to keep it clean once it's been circumcised."

"How would you know?"

Kleinpoppen did not want to go into the history of his penis. When he was sixteen, the family surgeon had removed his foreskin because warts had developed at the base of his glans, painful, fiery red welts that oozed pus and bled. Later, when he converted to Judaism to marry Judy, a mohel had performed a token circumcision—a *Hatafat Dam Brit* as opposed to a *Brit Milah*. The mohel had sprayed a local anesthetic on the loose flesh where the original cut had been made and then lanced the skin to extract a drop of blood at the place of the Milah, reciting the ancient prayers as he did so. Alice's question brought these memories flooding back up, choking the gutter of his emotions. What could he say? Anger came over him, and he decided all at once not to invite her to Andrew's bris.

"Believe me, I know."

"In Europe they don't circumcise boys," Alice said.

"Oh yeah?" Kleinpoppen wondered where she got this information, if it were true, and he also felt contempt burn through him at the blind reverence for European culture, as if it were self-evident that Europe was more civilized than America. The gentle Europeans.

"That's right. I will say that mohels are probably more humane than regular surgeons, more skilled. When Jerome was born and I was considering circumcision, I contacted a mohel. They are specialists, after all."

"Your son's not circumcised?"

Alice hesitated at the personal question. "No, he's not," she said finally.

* * *

"Another son would be fine," Kleinpoppen answered Debbie Goodman, a colleague of Judy's whom she'd invited, "but a daughter would be fine, too. I want to get Andy launched before we think of having another baby, though. I'm sure Judy feels the same."

They looked over at Judy. She seemed exhausted, sitting in a rocking chair nursing the newborn. At this moment, having another baby was probably the least appealing prospect in the world to her.

All of the guests had arrived, and they were just waiting for the mohel to make his appearance before they got underway with the bris. Marilyn Felser was giving instructions to the girl from the caterer's about the arrangement of food and plates on the table. She was wielding a cheese knife, and Kleinpoppen remembered his earlier thought about cutting her tongue out, with a reflexive sense of shame.

Actually, he was feeling a little guilty. More than once his mother-in-law's eyes had sought his, full of warmth and congratulation. Marilyn did not know he had overheard her outburst to Judy. He ignored her. He snubbed her. Cut her. She looked a little hurt and confused, he'd noticed with vindictive satisfaction.

The doorbell buzzed, and Kleinpoppen went out to the hallway to answer it. Through the frosted glass window pane he saw a tall, gaunt figure in a fedora. Must be the mohel. Seen this way, the mohel appeared to be a necessary stock character in a play. The Grim Reaper with his scythe? The welcoming angel. The gravedigger, the clown. A man without a name.

Kleinpoppen opened the door to Rabbi Fisher, a white-bearded man in his fifties with a gentle smile and gold wirerim glasses. Kindness radiated from the lines around his eyes. He wore a dark suit, and in his left hand he held a little case containing his instruments. With his right he shook hands with Kleinpoppen, stepping into the hallway.

"Come in, come in," Kleinpoppen welcomed the mohel. Showtime.

* * *

Like a stage performance indeed, a small table had been set up by the pantry door in the dining room, facing out on the rest of the room. On this table the mohel arranged his equipment. The dining table had been moved to the side of the room and the luncheon placed on the table. The guests came into the dining room to witness the ceremony.

"Among Jews, the Brit Milah is the oldest single ceremony continuously practiced," Fisher began in a benign, conversational tone. "Indeed, among all cultures it may be the most ancient, consistently practiced tradition. It signifies the welcoming of a new member into our Jewish community. Of course, Andrew has been a Jew since his birth," he said with a mild irony that elicited a chuckle from the assembled guests, "but he enters into the Covenant with God today, the eighth day of his life, as mandated in the Torah."

Judy's brother Ben and his wife, Yael, had agreed to be the *Sandek* and *Kvaterin*—the godfather and godmother—and Yael brought the swaddled baby into the room and handed him over to Ben, as was the prescribed custom. Then she went to stand beside Judy.

It was an odd choreography, Kleinpoppen thought, like a play in a football game diagramed on the blackboard and practiced over and over again. After Yael handed the baby off to Ben, Ben handed him to Kleinpoppen, who in turn handed him to the mohel. Touchdown. Then Kleinpoppen took his place beside Judy and Yael, facing the mohel, at right angles to the audience. He could see all their faces.

"What follows may not be appropriate for young children," the mohel advised, again in a mildly ironic tone. "Parental discretion is advised."

Several young children were herded out of the mohel's presence, and Fisher went about preparing the child for the cut, securing Andrew's legs in a little straitjacket sort of arrangement so he wouldn't squirm, clamping and snapping with precision his antiseptic stainless steel instruments. Then he recited the prayer: "*Barukh ata Adonai Elohenu Melech ha-olam asher kid-shanu b'mitzvotav vetzivanu al ha-Milah.*"

Immediately afterward he performed the operation, not that Kleinpoppen was able to see anything, as closely as he watched. It was over quickly, and Andrew yelped in pain. Sure, he felt it, no doubt about that. Judy almost swooned at the sound of her son's cry.

Then the Kleinpoppens chanted their prayer: "*Barukh ata Adonai Elohenu Melech ha-olam asher kid-shanu b'mitzvotav vetzivanu khakhniso bab'rito shel Avraham Avinu.*"

Kleinpoppen looked down at his son's squalling face, pinched in pain, wrinkled and red. He looked over at the audience and saw his mother-in-law. She, too, was crying, overcome with emotion, and in that instant Kleinpoppen was sure he recognized his son's features in Marilyn Felser. He felt a rush of compassion and forgiveness.

* * *

Kleinpoppen spread cream cheese with chives on a sliced poppyseed bagel, speared some lox and whitefish onto his plate, along with a slice of tomato, and he walked over to where his mother-in-law stood, chewing on her own bagel.

"Mazel tov," Marilyn Felser said to her son-in-law, happy to see that he was no longer avoiding her. Perhaps he had just been preoccupied, she decided.

"Well, mazel tov to you, too. You know, Marilyn, I looked over at you right after the mohel performed the bris, and I swear you and Andrew look so much alike."

"Really?" Marilyn beamed; she felt proud.

"The way his face scrunched when he was crying. It looked just like you."

Marilyn smiled magnificently at her son-in-law. "Well, I'll tell you, Robert. I hope Andrew gets your strong jaw," she said, "and I really hope he has your blue eyes."

The Hebrew Lesson

"I don't want to go to camp," Leah whined. The muggy summer had started, and it sapped everybody's energy. "I want to stay home."

Kleinpoppen finished snapping her into her carseat. She was old enough and big enough not to have to sit in one, but as long as she didn't complain, Kleinpoppen was just as happy to have her in it. It was safer. Besides, the backseat of his junky little Toyota Tercel was a mess after accommodating two children from infancy on. A litterbin of wrappers, crumbs, shells, lollipop sticks, stale candy. Andy sat in the front passenger's seat, inert with morning fatigue, his bare legs, in shorts, a little goosepimply with the morning coolness.

"Well, I've got to go to work, and so you've got to go to camp. I can't just let you stay home. I'd get arrested." It was like this most mornings, and he certainly remembered those feelings of resentment from his own childhood in Potawatomi Rapids. *Why? Why do I have to go to school?* It was a game, like the "which would you rather do?" game or the "what if" game.

"No, you wouldn't," Andy said, awakening to the challenge. "You'd just get fired."

"If I let you stay home by yourselves?"

"No, you'd stay home with us."

"Well, then I *would* get fired. You're right."

"So what? It's only a job."

"Yeah, but it pays for the clothes you wear and the food you eat. We'd all go hungry if I didn't go to work and do my job and get paid."

"Well, then why don't you get a restaurant job?" The game

of argumentation enchanted him.

"Why?"

"Then you'd be able to eat there. At the restaurant."

"If I worked at a restaurant, you'd still have to go to camp. So why don't we just avoid that hassle and I'll go to work at the job I already have, and you and Leah will go to the camp."

Andy and Leah were going to the Jewish Community Center summer camp out in the country. Kleinpoppen drove them to the JCC on Park Heights Avenue and left them there to take a schoolbus out to the camp with the other kids. It was mostly recreational, swimming and boating and so on, but there was some Jewish culture instruction as well.

"I *hate* shemesh!" Leah said petulantly.

"Shemesh? Isn't that the Hebrew word for 'sun?'"

"Very good, Dad," Andy said in the voice of a first grade teacher. Already, his knowledge of Hebrew far outstripped Kleinpoppen's. He attended a Jewish day school during the rest of the year. Kleinpoppen started a new game.

"And what is summer?"

"*Kayitz.*"

"And what is...winter?"

"*Choref.*"

"And what is...rain?"

"Rain is *geshem*. Water is *mayim*."

"Oh yeah?" Kleinpoppen looked over at Andy, proud of his knowledge, and then back at the road.

Andy did not respond, and after a moment Kleinpoppen resumed the game.

"And what is...sky?"

"*Shamayim.*"

"And what is...dirt?"

Andy thought. "*Adamah.*"

"And what is—"

"I don't want to play this any more!"

"Sorry."

Andy repented. "Why don't you just learn it yourself?"

"Hebrew? I don't want to." It was an ugly language to Kleinpoppen's ears. He had no desire to learn it or speak it. He only had a kind of abstract desire to keep up with his children and to know what they knew. They passed the Pimlico Racecourse on Northern Parkway.

"Look at the horses!" Kleinpoppen said, and Andy and Leah craned their necks to see the jockeys riding the horses around the track. Some cantered, some trotted.

"I see one!" Leah cried.

"Well I see *two!*" Andy one-upped her. Another morning commute competition.

* * *

"God, I think I'm going to have this smell all over my hands all summer," Kleinpoppen said to Janice when he signed in.

"What smell you gonna have all over your hands?" Ev Baker said, popping his head into Janice's cubicle, already laughing at his sexual innuendo. Kleinpoppen wondered if what he found so annoying about Baker was that his jokes were so lame and predictable or that Baker thought they were so clever and original. Two sides of the same coin.

"Sunscreen. Had to lather the kids up before I took them to camp."

"You see in the paper where some kid got shot at a public swimming pool?" Baker sat in the spare chair of Janice's cubicle like a paperweight; he was not about to move any time soon.

"Some other kid was shot to death while he was making a call at a public phone booth. Teenager."

"Was he black?" Baker's eyes glittered malevolently.

"Probably. Happened on the west side."

"What gets me," Baker said, "is that woman who left her kids in a car with the windows rolled up while she was partying with ten guys in a motel room and passed out, and the kids died."

"Oh, I saw that," Janice said, horrified.

"Passed out. They must have been gang-bangin' her." A leer passed over Baker's features, replaced by a look of righteousness. "They ought to do the same thing to her. Shut her up in a car in the desert and let her see how it feels."

Nobody said anything to that, and after a pause, Baker pursued his thought.

"I mean it. They ought to. Like those black kids a couple years ago who tried to carjack that woman's car with the baby in it, and they dragged her to death down the street. They should punish them the same way, let them see what it feels like. Drag them down the street behind a car. I bet they wouldn't do that again." His self-righteousness was like something solid, something you could lean on, a familiar archetypal thing, like a tree or a mountain.

"Well, yeah, sure, it sounds like what we'd all like to have happen, but it's a little barbaric, wouldn't you say?" Kleinpoppen spoke reluctantly. He hated being dragged into these stupid hypothetical arguments.

"Well it's what *you* believe," Baker said.

"What *I* believe?"

"Sure, an eye for an eye. The Jews believe in an eye for an eye. It's in the Bible. Aren't you Jewish?"

"I doubt that anybody these days would interpret that quite so literally, take it so literally as what justice is all about." Baker had gone straight for his identity. Who he was. A low blow. And not only his own self-conception, but Baker's interpretation of some larger category into which Kleinpoppen was supposed to fit. Fitting into somebody else's definition of the word "Jewish."

"Justice should be swift and sure. You don't punish a child for something it did wrong a week later. You punish it right away, so it knows *why* it's being punished."

"What about due process?"

"They have it on videotape! They drug her in her own car! It's right there on videotape! How much proof do you want?"

"I thought we were talking about the woman who left her kids in the car." Kleinpoppen looked for a way out. He did not like this discussion. Baker had a way of presenting himself as the defender of the innocent.

"Well there again. What was she doing in a motel room with ten other guys? Why'd she leave her kids out there to die?"

"Yeah, sure." What else was there to say?

"Yeah, sure," Baker repeated sarcastically. "You just don't let a child do something wrong and not punish them for it right away."

"This parent-child analogy only goes so far. Who's going to decide she gets punished, what her guilt is?"

"She neglected those kids. Those kids would be alive today if she didn't think of somebody else besides herself. You know why she couldn't bring those kids into the motel room. You know why she had to leave them in the car. None of those guys with her knew she had her kids with her. They just got her drunk and—" Baker caught himself, looked at Janice, then decided not to say it.

Why argue with the guy? Why bother? The fact was that nobody was going to punish this woman by shutting her up in a car in the desert, and even if they did, who cared? It was the kind of punishment Dante might have devised, let alone Baker.

"You Jews," Baker sneered. "You whine a lot about injustice, but only when it's against you." Baker launched himself out of his chair, nodded gallantly to Janice, and propelled himself out of the cubicle.

Kleinpoppen had the feeling he should have done something or said something. But what? Janice rolled her eyes at him and turned back to her computer screen.

Tzedakah, Kleinpoppen thought, going to his desk. The Hebrew word for "justice." It also meant "benevolence."

Another elemental concept to go along with earth, air, fire and water.

Hair and Share

A grizzled, shabby man in an old wornout overcoat sat by himself in the corner of the synagogue's recreation room, muttering to himself and looking around suspiciously. One of the city's homeless. Robert Kleinpoppen had seen him before. Ruddy, burly, with a thick, unwashed mane of red hair, he had the touchy, truculent manner of a stray dog.

When Kleinpoppen first met him, he'd adopted a Socratic skepticism as a sort of defensive strategy. He came to these potluck services to freeload, but he did it grudgingly. He was not about to show any gratitude. As a homeless person, he had seen more of life than the soft, cushy congregants, his attitude seemed to say, and he was not going to ingratiate himself to anybody.

"You aren't Jewish, are you?" he'd said to Kleinpoppen that first time, as if he were accusing him of fraudulence.

"I'm a convert."

"Why did you convert?" he demanded. His beady, red-streaked blue eyes narrowed with a kind of superiority. "Marriage, I suppose?"

Kleinpoppen decided not to engage him in conversation on these terms. He smiled and nodded at him, as if one of them were an idiot, and moved on to other people.

That must have been six months before. Now the man was back. Most people knew who he was and avoided him, the way you'd step around a churlish playground bully. But Josh, a new member, a law school student, made the mistake of greeting the man. Josh was new in town; he had joined for the fellowship as much as for his spiritual needs. He'd brought a friend with him, a blond woman, obviously a gentile.

"Only Jews are allowed to take part in the minyan," the beggar barked when Josh addressed him. It wasn't clear to Kleinpoppen if the man were Jewish or not. "You and your friend had better leave."

Mike Brooks overheard the exchange. Mike was a conservative man in his sixties, a self-made businessman, the kind of guy who has little sympathy for the less fortunate, whom he saw as having brought their misfortune upon themselves through laziness.

"You," he said to the homeless man, stabbing a finger at him. Mike was sturdy and squat, like a bantam streetfighter. "You get out of here if you aren't going to behave like a civilized human being."

"I don't have to!" The shabby man shrank away at the very opportunity he'd been seeking, to pick a fight.

"Go on. You heard me. Get out."

Several heads turned, and the president of the congregation, an attorney named Harold Baumgartner, tried to come between the two. He put his hand on the homeless man's arm.

"You're welcome to join us for services in the sanctuary."

"But he never joins. He just comes to eat and criticize."

"Okay, Mike." Harold turned back to the man, who seemed suddenly subdued, maybe even ashamed. Harold was a soft, fat man with a bushy black beard. "Okay? You understand? You're welcome to join us."

Meanwhile, Harold's wife, Sharon, tried to reassure Josh and his friend.

"This doesn't usually happen here," she said. Sharon was a gentle, diminutive woman with sharp, delicate features. "Most of the congregation here are very warm and friendly."

The thing that always stuck in Kleinpoppen's mind about Harold and Sharon Baumgartner was the names by which they referred to each other. Harold called his wife "Share," and she called him "Hair."

No, He's the Dumb One

Ev Baker hurried down the aisle to Romanchuck's office, an urgent look on his face. Janice, the secretary, was in Romanchuck's office talking to the boss. Robert Kleinpoppen was there, too, having just signed the daily log, and was about to go to his own cubicle.

"You hear about that couple out in the county?"

"What couple?"

"Seems this guy was throwing a surprise party for his wife. It's her thirtieth birthday and he wants it to be special. He buys a lot of food and drink and invites all their friends. He gets all the guests to come to his place early, and they all hide down in the basement. The guy even takes the dog with them so he won't go running around making noise and tearing into the cake and ripping up the decorations. Then the wife comes home from work, goes upstairs to change her clothes, and then she starts calling for the dog. She's calling everywhere, and the dog don't come because they've got him shut up down there in the basement with them, and then she comes down into the basement, and it's all dark and everything; all the lights are turned off and everything, and she's calling for the dog, and then she switches on the light, and everybody shouts, 'Surprise!' And there she is standing completely stark butt naked and she has a jar of peanut butter in her hand! Oh, man! Her husband was fit to be tied!"

"It's the truth," Janice said. "Dave says they got a call on a domestic down the station, and some of the officers had to investigate." Janice's husband was a police officer.

Romanchuck's face was red with laughter by this time. He clapped his hands. "Oh, my God!" he gasped.

"What was she doing with a jar of peanut butter?" Kleinpoppen asked, deadpan.

"What do you think?" Baker asked, disgusted. He'd missed Kleinpoppen's irony and took him for a sexual simpleton. Baker had this idea of himself as a sexual pioneer who had gone places no man had ever been.

"Oh, I get it. She was making a peanut butter and jelly sandwich," Kleinpoppen said. "For the dog."

Baker just shook his head and looked at Romanchuck. Some boobs were just too dumb to educate, his look said.

Kleinpoppen gave up and went to his cubicle to start the day's work, shaking his own head at Baker's obtuseness.

Family Secrets

Waiting for Judy to get the kids ready for the Rosh Hashanah service, Robert Kleinpoppen turned the television set on to kill time. One of those tabloid talkshows came on, the kind he missed by going to work every day. A woman with three names strutted around in the television audience with a mike in her hand. Rikki Tiki Tavi or something like that. A handsome, middleaged white woman with owllike eyeglasses that made her look intelligent, she reminded Kleinpoppen of the actresses who played business executives on infomercials for high tech software systems. A couple young kids on folding chairs on the stage faced the studio audience, he a swarthy, beefy young man with a mustache, she a young woman with more makeup than Mick Jagger. The topic: Women Who Get Pregnant to Trap Their Men.

So this was what the public television types were so upset about, the smutty, sensational exploitation of confused kids to satiate the public's appetite for dirty laundry, family secrets. Somehow it looked to Kleinpoppen about as authentic as professional wrestling. What was the big deal?

The mistress of ceremonies was crossexamining the girl like a public prosecutor.

"You said you were in love with him."

"No, I said I love him, not that I was *in* love with him."

"So you love him?"

"In a way yes, in a way no."

Kleinpoppen watched, transfixed. What did any of this *mean*? He could see himself and his first wife, Paula, as the guests on a show like this, seated up on stage in front of the cameras. Kleinpoppen's first wife was a Florida cracker who had dumped him for a defrocked born again evangelist, a bush league Jimmy Swaggert who'd been kicked out of his pulpit for sexual peccadillos with the congregation. Kleinpoppen had met Judy a year later and after a year of dating had converted to Judaism and married her. Judy was likewise on the rebound from an abusive marriage; her husband used to beat her until she was bloody and bruised. Come to think of it, Judy and Norman might very well be up on the stage, too. Or he and Judy. Topic: Interfaith Marriages: Can They Work? Topic: Conversion: Compromise or Betrayal? Or they could *all* be up there at once, spilling out the sordid details of their messy lives. Norman on a husband's prerogative to pound his wife; Paula on the preacher's prerogative to pound Kleinpoppen's wife.

Rikki Tiki Tavi continued her questions.

"But you were dating other men, weren't you? At least that's what Kevin claims."

"I went out a lot."

"You went out a lot?"

"Well, I did, but I didn't, you know?"

Suddenly Kevin, the beefy guy, started to harangue the girl, gesturing wildly with his arms, Italian style.

"You trapped me! She trapped me!" he said, turning to Rikki and the studio audience. "She told me she was using protection, man, and she wasn't using *no* protection!"

The girl's saucy retort: "Well *you* could have pulled out."

The audience tittered. Some even clapped. This was the kind of thing they were here for, after all.

Kleinpoppen glanced at his watch, wondering if they would be late for the Torah reading. Then he found himself wondering what it would be like to have Abraham and Sarah up there on the stage being questioned in front of a television audience.

"So you were jealous of your husband's mistress Hagar, and that's why you sent her packing along with her son, is that right, Sarah?"

"Well, I was and I wasn't, you know?"

"Were you afraid Ishmael might get Isaac's inheritance? What about the allegations that Ishmael buggered your son?"

"Well, there was that consideration, but that's not everything."

"That's not all?"

"Well, there was more."

"Like what?"

"Oh, there was this and there was that, you know?"

"And you, Abraham. You say you threatened your son with a knife because a voice told you to sacrifice him, and yet you didn't even bother to talk any of this over with your own wife, did you?"

"Well, I was going to. I thought about it. But as Kierkegaard said, faith isn't a rational proposition."

"Kierkegaard said that?"

"Well, he did, but he didn't, you know?"

"How do you think all this made Isaac feel? He was probably pretty traumatized, wouldn't you think?"

"Well, he was, but he wasn't, you know what I'm saying?"

Judy came clattering down the stairs with Andy and Leah, late as usual and all set to get going. The children, as yet uncomplicated by regrets, looked fresh and eager but close to the edge of a sulk.

"Here we go!" she said in a musical sing-song, trying to put a positive spin on it. "The rabbi's going to tell us a *won*derful story about our ancestors, Isaac and his Daddy and Mommy, Abraham and Sarah!"

Reluctantly, Kleinpoppen turned the set off. Talk about family secrets and modern moral dilemmas, he thought, reaching into his pocket for the car keys.

* * *

They arrived at the synagogue after the service had already

begun and only single seats remained. Kleinpoppen volunteered to take the children down to the rec. room where the children's service was being led by sprightly Donna Feltzer, a third grade teacher by profession who made the whole service seem like an episode of *Mister Rogers* or *Sesame Street*. It was likely to be less ponderous than Rabbi Shulman's service. Kleinpoppen found the rabbi too eager to show off his learning and wisdom, to flaunt his education and insight as a sort of implicit challenge, as if he were out to vanquish all foes on the field of Sagacity and Judgment. Words like "pretentious" and "pedantic" and "pompous" came to mind, but the one Kleinpoppen settled for was "boring." He wondered if this were an occupational hazard of being a spiritual leader.

"Chag Sameach," Kleinpoppen mumbled to Edith Naden, settling his children into seats.

"Good yom tov."

"Now who can tell me who Abraham was?" Donna Feltzer was asking, and immediately Kleinpoppen excused himself to go to the men's room. He went down a narrow corridor that made him think of clammy dungeons in horror movies, the drip of water audible from some unseen watertap. His children often told him they were frightened by the enormous black waterbugs they saw scurrying around down here.

In the men's room, Kleinpoppen heard voices and stood outside in the hallway to await his turn. Rabbi Shulman was talking to somebody whose voice Kleinpoppen did not recognize.

"We'll go down to the Jones Falls this afternoon for *Tashlikh*," Shulman said.

"*Tashlikh*," the unfamiliar voice said, putting the glottal Levantine emphasis on the final syllable, as if he were clearing his throat. "A quaint custom. The Romans had a similar ceremony to propitiate the pagan gods."

"Petrarch writes of a custom among the people of Cologne

who threw objects into the Rhine. That was in the fourteenth century. The Jewish ceremony may therefore originate in a Christian practice."

"It's been castigated as a superstition by some rabbis."

"But not by this one."

The other man chuckled with mock goodfellowship, but the hollow quality of his laughter really said, "Go to Hell" to the rabbi.

"What's key here is your concept of prayer. The Hebrew word, *hit-palayl*, has a much different meaning than the word as we commonly know it. 'Prayer' comes from the Middle English via the Old French and ultimately from the Latin word *precari*, meaning 'to entreat,' or 'to obtain through entreaty.'

"The Hebrew word focuses on the penitential feelings of the one who prays. The efficacy of the prayer is measured by how the penitent feels when he comes away from the prayer. The word does not equate to 'wish fulfillment,' as 'prayer' so often does.

"This concept of prayer is consistent with the whole period of *Teshuvah* that begins with Rosh Hashanah. *Teshuvah*, or Return to God, is a daily obligation; repentance is part of our three daily prayers, after all. But these High Holidays are designed to bring it to a pinnacle of fervor, Eugene, and 'quaint' or 'superstitious' as *Tashlikh* may seem to modern man, the idea behind it is to cleanse ourselves. A symbolic gesture."

"I thought the Hebrew word for prayer was *tefillah*," Eugene said, standing toe to toe with the rabbi in an exchange of Hebrew scholarship.

"The noun, yes. The verb is *hit-palayl*. Same root."

The toilet flushed, and the bathroom door opened. Eugene Shulman, the rabbi's brother from Saint Louis, came out ahead of the rabbi, who was fumbling with something in the pocket of his suit jacket. It looked to Kleinpoppen like a flask, though it could have been a prayerbook, he thought. Both men nodded at Kleinpoppen and muttered a Chag Sameach and proceeded down the hallway to the sanctuary. Kleinpoppen thought he caught a tang of whiskey in the air. Rabbi Shulman, a shikker? Nah, couldn't be, could he? Sneaking drinks with his brother in the synagogue men's room? No way.

The Ultimate Checkmate

Robert Kleinpoppen decided to buy his eight-year old son, Andy, a chess set for Chanukah. He'd been inspired by a piece on "All Things Considered" about some kids in a Chicago slum who had started a chess club and among the results their grades had improved dramatically. The reporter interviewed an educational expert who talked about how chess develops logical skills and improves rational processes. You thought not only about moves but overall game plans to trap the king. You learned to think five moves in advance, the expert said. Not that Andy was having any difficulty in school, but it couldn't hurt. Besides, he had to provide his son with a gift for eight nights running, and here was one.

But Andy didn't seem that thrilled when he ripped the festive wrapping of dancing dreidels and lit menorahs from the package, especially since his younger sister, Leah, who had recently turned five, received a "Toobers and Zots" set that intrigued him more. Other people's toys always hold great charm. When he tried to take it away from her to play with it himself, Leah cried out, and Kleinpoppen and his wife had to intervene. The customary sibling conflict ensued. Sometimes Kleinpoppen wished he could foresee these situations developing and have a strategy at hand to defuse them, five moves ahead.

Kleinpoppen had picked up a free copy of *Healthy KIDS* at the pediatrician's office when he'd brought Andy and Leah in for their annual checkup the week before, a slick publication with smiling children on the cover and an optimistic tone. A featured article asked, "Can You Stop Sibling Rivalry?" But when he looked inside, he saw it was "Ten Surefire Ways to

Encourage Brotherly (and Sisterly) Love." Cutesy. Like the housekeeping journals in the grocery. Ten ways to save your marriage, six tips for fashion success and four strategies for losing weight, a redecorating plan as easy as one-two-three.

"You love her more than you love me!" Andy accused Judy.

"Don't be silly. I love you both the same."

"Well she got a better present than I did!"

"Better than chess?" Kleinpoppen cried. "You'll *love* that chess set, Andy, once you learn how to play!"

Andy grumbled. "Well at least she ought to share."

"Leah, why don't you and Andy make something together with those Toobers and Zots," Judy said, trying to negotiate a compromise. The Toobers and Zots had come mail order from the Metropolitan Museum of Art. It consisted of malleable tubes and geometric shapes that you could put together to make animals and buildings. A creative toy. A parent's nightmare of a million tiny, fragile pieces that would inevitably get lost under furniture or crushed underfoot.

"But it's mine!" Leah said defensively. She was suspicious of her big brother, who had a way of taking things over when they "shared."

Losing patience, Kleinpoppen played his trump card. "All right, *nobody* gets to play with these toys, the Toobers and Zots *or* the chess set! And we aren't giving you any presents the rest of Chanukah, either!" Dad as ogre tyrant.

Both children cried out in alarm and started to play together with the Toobers and Zots.

"I'll teach you how to play chess this weekend, Andy, okay?"

* * *

Kleinpoppen worked as a technical writer on a software support contract with the federal government. The federal workers had been furloughed more than a week earlier because of the Congressional budget impasse. Lately, Kleinpoppen had been coming to work with little to do but listen to speculation on the Congressional maneuvering and the political posturing of the President and his rivals. It didn't help that the election was less than a year away and primary season about to begin.

"They're not going to let him go this time," Kleinpoppen's boss, George Romanchuk, said. "They gave him a continuing resolution last time when he promised to come up with a balanced budget, and he didn't. They're going to hold his feet to the fire on this."

"Well, it doesn't make them look very good, all these furloughed federal workers and the government services shutting down," Ron Umerlik said. Ron was a federal employee who was continuing to work though not getting paid.

"Already I understand the CDC isn't able to collect the data they need for developing a flu vaccine for next fall," somebody else put in. "The American people are going to hold Congress responsible for that come the next election." The usual group of half a dozen people had gathered by the photocopier to air their views.

"That's all Clinton cares about," Romanchuk maintained, a partisan Republican to the end. "He sees he's getting the benefit of the polls, but he don't care about the federal workers or everybody else who's taking it in the neck."

"You think the others care? You think *any* of those politicians give a damn?"

"Politicians! They haven't got the courage of a snake! Instead of taking a stand for the good of all, they listen to the lobbyists who give them money."

"It's us federal workers who are the pawns in their game."

"That Clinton's a smart one. He snared the Republicans into focusing on Medicare cuts, so he could *look* like he was taking a stand, make them all look greedy about their tax cut."

So they argued back and forth, pundits analyzing the strategies of the different political parties. Kleinpoppen rarely participated in these discussions. Not that he didn't have an opinion, but he preferred to listen to the others instead.

* * *

When he wasn't engaged in the endless debates about the budget crisis, Kleinpoppen was working on the synagogue's newsletter. He'd become editor that fall, a job he had been unable to wriggle out of when it had been offered to him. Each month, he published the calendar of upcoming events, acknowledgements of donations, congratulations for births and weddings, condolences for deaths and illness. The rabbi and the president of the congregation contributed a column, and Kleinpoppen often wrote a book review.

But now the conflict between the rabbi, Alan Shulman, and the Board of Directors had finally come to a head. For years they had been unable to get along together. Shulman considered himself the final authority on matters of religious observance, and several of the board members found his attitude annoying. Shulman seemed to disregard their opinions, to claim more authority than they wanted to grant with regard to synagogue policies and religious prohibitions. They regarded the rabbi as their employee and demanded a more ingratiating demeanor. Shulman had his loyal following among the congregation, but when his contract came up for renewal, the board decided not to offer him another year. In his column, Marvin Cohen, the president, diplomatically reported that the board had accepted Shulman's resignation; he said how much everybody appreciated what the rabbi had done for the congregation and wished him well in his future endeavors on behalf of the larger Jewish community.

Of course, everybody knew Shulman had been canned, and Kleinpoppen had received several letters from congregants complaining about the shabby way the rabbi had been treated and objecting that they had not been consulted. Kleinpoppen did not want to publish the letters. He did not want the newsletter to become the forum for recriminating debate over the rabbi. So he developed a strategy for explaining the board's strategy to the letter writers in order to circumvent their anger at his refusal to print their letters.

"You and I both know Shulman's getting shafted," he told Edith Naden over the phone. Hers had been the shrillest, demanding a re-evaluation, a meeting of the whole congregation. Her letter had hinted at a grass roots petition drive. "But we'd be doing the rabbi a disservice if we printed your letter. The whole Jewish community in Baltimore will know about it, and if it gets out that he was dumped, it might give him the appearance of being damaged goods. Then he'd have an even harder time getting another position. It's kind of like the Cleveland Browns, you know? The citizens of Cleveland can complain all they want, but the Browns are coming to Baltimore. No amount of effort on our part is going to bring Rabbi Shulman back.

"Besides, the rabbi *did* offer his resignation. He saw he wasn't getting along with the board, as much as he liked the rest of us, and he figured it was time to move on."

"Well, I wish there was something we could do," Edith said, surrendering.

So it appeared Kleinpoppen's strategy was paying off. Maybe he should offer his advice to the people in Washington.

* * *

On the drive home that evening, "All Things Considered" aired another story on chess. This one featured a Grand Master talking about the Harvard Cup Human Versus Computer Chess Challenge taking place in New York. He spoke confidently about humans being superior to the machines. Sometimes the computer's moves were so obvious, he said, that it would bring a smile to your lips. But he agreed you could not become too complacent.

The interviewer probed. One day the computer really would be able to "think," and would mankind give way to the thinking machine? Would human intelligence one day simply be no match for the computer?

"They have difficulty evaluating one position against another," the Grand Master said, but he conceded, "Computers are great on defense when you put the pressure on them." Kleinpoppen began to feel nervous. What if machines really were about to surpass humans in intelligence? It was like some weird Orwellian nightmare. The ultimate checkmate.

He pulled into his driveway just as the Grand Master mentioned the most sophisticated artificial intelligence program yet developed, IBM's "Deep Blue," was challenging the world champion of chess, Gary Kasparov, later in the year, and some experts predicted the computer would win. We have to remain vigilant, Kleinpoppen thought, alarmed. He resolved to show Andy how to play chess that evening.

"Andy!" Kleinpoppen set his briefcase and newspaper down, took off his coat. He heard the tumble of small feet coming down the stairs. Andy and Leah were on winter vacation from school.

"Did you bring us a treat?" both children asked.

"No treat, but I'd like to start in on the chess if you're up for it, Andy." He watched the incipient frown begin to crease the child's face.

"Oh, man!" Leah pouted. There was nothing in it for her. Kleinpoppen tried to remember the ten surefire ways to solve the sibling rivalry crisis. *Establish consistent rules of behavior. Don't take sides. Don't try to make everything equal. Redirect your child's energies...*

For Andy, Leah's response had the effect of making chess seem all at once an attractive prospect.

"Leah, why don't you watch, too. Come on. I'll get you both some apple juice. Andy, go get the set."

Both children seemed pleased with this arrangement. Had Kleinpoppen followed the steps correctly? Or was he just a natural born diplomat? Maybe he *should* offer his services to the government after all.

"Okay, which do you want, the black or the white?"

"Black!"

"White gets to move first."

"Then I'll be white! I want to go first!"

"Okay, now line them up this way, putting the Queen on her color."

Kleinpoppen showed Andy how to line the pieces up, naming each one and demonstrating the moves each piece was allowed to make.

"Why are there so many of these little ones? They're boring."

"Those are the pawns. Think of them as federal workers."

"What?"

"Think of them as the foot soldiers, the faceless little workers with very little power. The army of peasants or serfs."

"The Queen is the most powerful piece. She can go along the diagonals or back and forth along the ranks and files."

"Where's the Queen?" Leah asked. "The Queen's stronger than the King?"

"No she's not!" Andy cried impulsively. "The King is stronger than the Queen, isn't he Dad?"

"Well, not exactly."

"Yes he is."

"No he's not!"

Kleinpoppen smiled. "Well, the King is the most *important* piece. The object is to checkmate the King."

"Told ya."

"See, these are all representative of Medieval society. The King and Queen, the Knight, who's the official military man, the Castle, the Bishop."

"The Bishop? The Bishop's Christian, isn't he?"

"Well, yeah, but the piece doesn't have any religious significance, really, just represents the Church like some character out of *Canterbury Tales*."

"Why can't we call him the Rabbi? Where's the Rabbi?"

"Okay, let's call the Bishop the Rabbi," Kleinpoppen said. "Okay, the Rabbi can only go in a diagonal direction.

"Can I hold the Queen?"

"No, Leah, leave the pieces on the board, okay?"

"I want to play, too!"

"The Rabbi goes up and down the rows?"

"No, that's the Castle. The Rabbi is the one that moves diagonally."

"Why can't the Rabbi go whichever way he wants?"

"Because the Board of Directors doesn't want him to."

"What?"

"It's against the rules, that's all."

"Why can't I play, too, Dad?"

"This is my chess game, Leah, not yours!"

Kleinpoppen began to feel overwhelmed by the futility of trying to teach his children to play chess. They were about to fight again. Maybe he should shelve the game for a few years. Feeling the pressure, he went on the defense.

"Hey, I've got a good idea. Why don't we all play Candy Land?"

"Yeah!" The faces of both children brightened. Feeling triumphant, Kleinpoppen wondered if Deep Blue could ever have come up with *that* move.

Valhalla

"A Kodak moment." Robert Kleinpoppen nodded at the bride and groom standing with their wedding party, men in tuxedos, bridesmaids in matching purple gowns. The group was having its picture taken in front of Jacobs Field. The Kleinpoppens were on their way to the Rock and Roll Hall of Fame Museum at the other end of East Ninth Street. The August sky was blue, perfect for travel and photography. They'd come up with the plan to stop in Cleveland on their way from Baltimore to Potawatomi Rapids for their summer vacation a year before. Originally an inspiration, the plan had become more like a challenge by this time, however, like a dare. They could have made it as far as Ann Arbor by nightfall, they knew, but they'd reserved a room in a Ramada Inn in Cleveland, so they felt stuck.

The Rock and Roll Hall of Fame Museum in the glass pyramid on the Lake Erie shore turned out to be as big a disappointment as they'd feared. Perhaps it was all a self-fulfilling prophecy. Maybe, coming to it all skeptical and cynical, they'd set themselves up for a let-down. But the treatment seemed superficial, little more than photographs and clips of Grammy Awards ceremonies and MTV videos.

The Kleinpoppens stayed about an hour and a half, Andy and Leah whining to leave after the first thirty minutes. The two children worshipped the Beatles, enchanted by the latest Fab Four Revival, and most of the displays were of personalities they'd never heard of. The Velvet Underground? Alan Freed? Sam Phillips?

When they emerged from the Rock and Roll Museum, there was the wedding entourage, purple bridesmaids and all, arranging themselves for another photo session in front of the glass pyramid.

"Boy, we were had," Judy said, laughing.

"Well, I'm glad we came," Kleinpoppen said, aiming for the positive spin. "At least we can say we've been here."

"Only, I don't think I'll tell anybody; I'd be too embarrassed! What a rip. Forty-five bucks for that? It makes me ashamed to be a baby boomer."

"Okay, I'll agree that they could have done something a little more thorough or substantial with the subject than just rock star idolatry. A little more by way of analysis and historical development. Influences. But after all, it *is* like a monument. A lot of people probably feel the same letdown at the Vietnam War Memorial."

"Face it, Bob. They suckered us with boomer nostalgia, the way they do every few years with the Beatles. When we got to the Hall of Fame lobby I felt like I was at the circus being fasttalked by some carny into plunking down a quarter to go into the 'Paradise' exhibit."

"It wasn't that bad."

They walked down to the harbor by the Great Lakes Science Center and sat on a bench. The lake was as placid as the sky, and several yachts were cruising around on the water.

"I'm sure Graceland and the Grand Ole Opry are no different," Kleinpoppen went on.

"You ever get into country music?"

"A little. Until the guys with the big hats took over. I used to like the steel guitar tunes, the sad lyrics about the girl who stole the lonely cowpoke's heart."

"Ever notice how in rock and roll songs they always promise to buy the girl a diamond ring?"

"An obsession with money."

"But it's like a payoff. There's no real security."

"Well, what do you think?" Kleinpoppen improvised a lyric:

*I'll buy you a mutual fund
I'll buy you a mutual fund
I'll buy you a mutual fund
If you'll just let me dance with you."*

The children had been pestering them to go to the motel so they could get into the swimming pool. A tone of desperation had crept into their insistence; everybody was tired. So Judy and Robert got off the bench and went to the parking lot to retrieve their car.

*I'll pay for your children's education
I'll pay for your children's education
I'll pay their college expenses and tuition
If you'll only let me take you home*

On Ninth Street, the bride and groom were going by in an open white convertible, a handful of the purple bridesmaids beside them, a "JUST MARRIED" sign on the back. The bride waved to no one, as if she were in a parade, but nobody on the street paid her any attention.

"God," Kleinpoppen said. "Another Kodak moment."

* * *

"So how was the Rock and Roll Museum?" Uncle Alvin asked. They were sitting on Eleanor Kleinpoppen's front porch listening to the waves roll in from the lake. Her younger brother had come over as soon as he heard her son and family had arrived. Alvin had always struck his nephew as a sort of excited little watchdog yapping endlessly at passersby.

"It was okay."

"It was terrible," Judy corrected. "A real waste of time. We could have been here last night if we hadn't decided to go there."

Uncle Alvin laughed. "So you spent the night in Cleveland? God, what a desolate place. I remember when it was a joke. Before the PR guys and the urban developers went to work. Like that pissant town you live in, Baltimore."

After all this time, Alvin's remarks no longer registered on Kleinpoppen. He no longer rose to the bait. Sure, he could slam dunk Alvin with some sarcastic remark about the cosmopolitan standards of Potawatomi Rapids residents, but what was the use? "At an overpriced Ramada Inn down the road from a honkytonk that advertized X-rated videos and nude women wrestling in creamed corn."

"Sounds delicious."

"Actually, we had dinner at a Pizza Hut."

"Pizza Hut," Alvin repeated derisively. Judy and Robert exchanged amused looks, and then they sank into silence, hypnotized by the sound of the waves hitting the shore.

"Mosquitoes have been bad this year. Big as horseflies, and ferocious as hell. It's on account of the rain."

"We've had a cool summer in Baltimore," Judy said. "Lots of rain there, too."

"I know. You get our weather a day or two later."

"Not always," Kleinpoppen said, unable to resist the urge to contradict his uncle. He seemed to be implying that their experience was derivative, only an echo. "Sometimes—"

"Yeah, yeah, I know. Storms come up the coast from the Gulf. But on the whole, the prevailing weather patterns go from west to east. So, you staying for Aunt Nikki's memorial service on Sunday?"

As if on cue, Eleanor Kleinpoppen pushed open the screen door and came out onto the porch. She was dressed in jeans, a sweater, and running shoes.

"Ellie and I are expected to go, of course. I don't suppose you have to go if you don't want to."

Torn between an impulse to poke holes in his uncle's conception of his own importance and an inclination to take the loophole, Kleinpoppen said nothing.

"Nikki's memorial service?" Eleanor Kleinpoppen said. "They specifically requested no children, so at least one of you will have to stay behind with Andy and Leah."

"Who's 'they'?"

"Sue and Nancy." Nikki's children.

"It's one of those Quaker deals where people speak when they're moved to it." Alvin's tone was cynical as always. "Nancy's idea, I think."

Kleinpoppen looked at his mother. In the two years since his father had died she'd regained her composure and was actually in much better shape, physically—stronger, not as heavy.

"Well, we'll think about it. We have several days to decide, don't we? Meanwhile, I think we'll take Andy and Leah to Sleeping Bear tomorrow."

"Would you like to stay for dinner tonight?" Eleanor Kleinpoppen asked her brother.

"Sounds good to me!" Alvin turned to Kleinpoppen and Judy. "Sleeping Bear! That's at least an hour's drive, almost two!" He sounded incredulous and he looked annoyed. "I'd think after all that driving you'd be sick of cars!"

* * *

"It's just that it looked overcast yesterday," Kleinpoppen protested, to his wife's amusement. "I wasn't intimidated by Uncle Alvin. If I took everything he said to heart I probably wouldn't get out of bed in the morning."

"Well, it's overcast now, and the kids sure gave me a hard time when we didn't go. They expected to go to Sleeping Bear yesterday."

"What's the hurry? We're here now, aren't we?" They pulled into the Philip Hart visitors center in Empire. The park headquarters. "You guys want to get out?"

Andy and Leah spilled out of the backseat, and they all went into the visitors center. They looked at the museum pieces, ancient Indian watercraft, pictures of old lighthouses, samples of grass and sand. There was a slideshow in the visitors center that described the geological processes that had resulted in the sand dunes, the glaciers that moved across the land during the Ice Age millions of years before.

The slideshow narrator went on to describe the four categories of dunes—beach, perched, falling and de-perched. The authoritative voice explained the process of dune migration, generally toward the northeast at Sleeping Bear because of prevailing southwesterly winds, the mineral composition of the local sand—quartz—notable for its resistance to physical and chemical breakdown, and the plants that grow on the dunes—beachgrass, sand cherry and cottonwood. Natural processes that took generations and generations.

They went back to the car after the slideshow. Andy looked groggy and Leah had actually fallen asleep.

"That slideshow reminded me of the factoid hours they have on PBS, with the comforting voice of the narrator telling you about the mating habits of tortoises in the Galapagos Islands," Judy said. "It was great. It almost put me to sleep."

"It sure knocked Leah out." Kleinpoppen lowered their daughter into her seat. "Okay, what say we take in the Pierce Stocking Scenic Drive and then have lunch?"

"Sounds good to me."

Kleinpoppen caught the reference to Uncle Alvin and laughed. "He used to give my father a hard time. All those years together in Potawatomi Rapids with his wife's unmarried kid brother snapping and barking. They'd met in college at Northwestern. I guess he got used to Alvin."

"Like you get used to a sand dune. What's his last name, again?"

"Hudson. There were the three of them, Uncle Alvin, Aunt Nikki, and mom."

"And Nikki married the Chicago banker."

"Nikki collected influential people. Politicians, artists, academics. The opinion-makers. She had a world class art collection that she bequeathed to a number of museums."

"She must have been pretty wealthy."

Remembering the song they'd improvised in Cleveland, Kleinpoppen added a new verse:

You had nothin' when I met you, baby,
But look what you got now.
IRAs, financial plans,
Stocks on the NASDAQ and the Dow.

"How old was she?"

"Eighty-seven. She was the oldest."

"She died last winter?"

"February. Lymphoma. They had a similar service in Phoenix, where she lived, but I guess Uncle Alvin and my mother thought one would be appropriate in Potawatomi Rapids when the summer resort people who remembered her would be here."

"You going to go?"

Kleinpoppen made a quick decision. "I ought to accompany my mother."

"I'll take the kids to the beach."

They stopped the car at the dune overlook and got out of the car. They were on the eastern edge of the sand dunes now, on top of one of the tallest dunes—a perched dune, as far as Kleinpoppen could figure—as high as 200 feet above the lake. The wind was strong, and they had to close their eyes against it. The sand when it hit bare flesh, and Leah woke up, disoriented and cranky. A trail of wooden planks coiled and undulated across the ground onto the dune. They walked across the planks to different viewing platforms, from which they could make out North and South Manitou Islands, Pyramid

Point, Glen Lake, Sleeping Bear Bay and the Sleeping Bear Dunes.

"You didn't bring the camera!" Judy shouted over the howling wind.

"I guess since my father died I've kind of lost interest in photography," Kleinpoppen shouted back by way of apology. "Pictures don't really capture the things you really want to keep, I guess."

They continued on their hike around the national park. At the highest viewing platform they all huddled together on a bench and looked out into Lake Michigan, down the steep slope to the shore where tiny human figures hundreds of feet below crawled along by the water like ants. The sun shone in a cloudless sky. The wind gusted even more forcefully.

"Those are the bear cubs out there." Kleinpoppen pointed to the two islands. "North Manitou and South Manitou." He had to shout to be heard over the wind.

"How does the story go, again? The Indian myth of Sleeping Bear?" Judy asked. "Tell Andy and Leah. They didn't get into it much in the slideshow."

Kleinpoppen ducked his head into the wind to find the pocket of still air around them on the bench, and he related the story to his enchanted children. Usually Judy read them stories, but this was one Kleinpoppen knew from his childhood.

"There was this mother bear the Indians called Mishe-Mokwa. My Chippewa isn't too good, but I know 'mokwa' means bear. Anyway, she had two cubs. This was on the Wisconsin side of Lake Michigan, before there were many humans around, and the bears frolicked happily in the forest and led untroubled bear lives. Mishe-Mokwa would take her little cubs down to the shore of the lake and they'd splash around.

"One night there was this terrific thunderstorm, and lightning struck the dry trees, starting a huge forest fire. The woods went up like matchsticks. Mishe-Mokwa hustled her cubs to the lake, and they started to swim. The whole shoreline was a single blaze of flame, and they swam out and out into the deep water. They swam all night and all the next day, and pretty soon the cubs started falling behind. Mishe-Mokwa urged them to continue, but then another huge storm came along and separated them completely, even though they all continued to swim. Mishe-Mokwa swam through the night and all the next day, and just as the third night began, she spotted land. Worn out, she made it to the shore and lay there waiting for the cubs. But they didn't come and didn't come, and she lay there grieving, not wanting to leave for fear the cubs would come when she was gone.

"The cubs had drowned, of course, but she had no way of knowing that. The great spirit Manitou saw all this with great sadness, and he took Mishe-Mokwa into the great, endless spirit Universe. After she died, Manitou raised the two cubs and made them into the two islands which he named after himself because of the great faithfulness of Mishe-Mokwa. North Manitou and South Manitou. Manitou covered the sleeping bear with mounds of sand and said—" Kleinpoppen made his voice a deep, godlike baritone— "'From this day on, as you wait resting, all men will know you as The Sleeping Bear, and they will all know of your goodness and patience.'"

"So those two islands out there are the cubs? For real?" Andy and Leah were willing to believe it with a child's imagination.

"My mother said her mother used to say she and Uncle Alvin were the twin cubs," Kleinpoppen told his wife. "Her mother said it seemed she spent her whole life just waiting for them. At the dentist's, at the doctor's, at school, at the playground, waiting for them to wake up, to go to sleep, to finish eating. Just waiting. For them."

* * *

"Enjoying your vacation?" Uncle Alvin asked. They were sitting in the piney clearing behind what had been Nikki's summer cottage by the lake. The ground was thick with needles and seemed to muffle the sound, an impression reinforced by the muted, constant sound of the lake, blocked by a line of massive pines that served as a windbreak.

"It's gone too fast. We're driving back to Baltimore tomorrow."

"You've had nice weather," Alvin said, as if his nephew had been complaining.

"Yeah, all except for the first day when it was kind of overcast."

"Well, you take what you get," Alvin said in a kind of philosophical summary, and then he greeted another guest who had just arrived for the service.

Kleinpoppen followed his mother to a row of chairs that had been set up beneath the high arching branches of the pines, so that there was a kind of amphitheater effect, with an audience and a stage. Aunt Nikki's two daughters, Sue and Nancy, women about a dozen years older than Kleinpoppen, whom he had never known very well, had made the arrangements for the service. A reception with punch and fruit, cheese and crackers would follow.

When the guests were all seated, Nancy thanked everybody for coming and asked for a moment of silent prayer. Then she suggested that anybody who felt moved to offer memories of her mother would be welcomed and encouraged to do so.

Uncle Alvin stepped forward first. He seemed to teeter on his feet, as if the slightest breeze would blow him away. He had never seemed so frail to Kleinpoppen.

"I grew up as the kid brother of two very different sisters," he started, and then he seemed to choke on the memory and the emotion. He took a moment to recover. "Mom and Pop moved here to Potawatomi Rapids from Chicago to join the firm Pop later led, before Potawatomi Rapids had been discovered by all the tourists and the summer resort crowd." He had a way of exaggerating the importance of the place.

"I was devoted to both my sisters, in different ways. Nikki I was proud of because she outdid us all, I guess you'd say. She was off to New York before I really ever got to know her that well. She was eleven years older than me, after all. Then she married Reynolds and they went all around the world all the time, and they'd send cards to me and Ellie. I liked to think that when she was here in Potawatomi Rapids, usually only for a few weeks every summer here in this magnificent cottage of hers, I liked to think she thought of herself as being at home, finally and undeniably home, and that home *was* a place she could go back to." Alvin seemed to forget what he was trying to say then, lost the track of his thought, and he tried to recover gracefully, but ultimately he could not.

"I guess after Reynolds died, Nikki kind of depended more on us, on Ellie and me. Like Ellie here after her husband Teddy died a couple years back." Alvin abruptly sat down then, and Kleinpoppen could sense a sort of confusion among the guests. He looked at Alvin for signs of grief or vacancy, but Alvin's expression was implacable, and then Kleinpoppen's mother was struggling up from her chair beside him and moving up to face the audience. She scuttled like a raccoon, all balance and caution.

In a low voice, Eleanor Kleinpoppen started to sing a song she had written to the tune of "Where Have All the Flowers Gone?" A recitation of those she'd lost, her parents, her husband, her brother-in-law, her sister. "Where has all my family gone?"

After Nikki's siblings, her children spoke of their mother's courage at the end, facing death, and then various friends spoke of her knowledge of art and her and Reynold's philanthropy. They were all frail, ancient people, Kleinpoppen saw, and any thoughts of speaking about his aunt were smothered under a thick blanket of humility. How self-serving it would have sounded!

After the service, a few old cronies came up to Eleanor Kleinpoppen and suggested that she record for posterity the song she had sung in her sister's honor. But Kleinpoppen's mother realized how trite and pathetic it would sound, out of context of the occasion, and her eyes shone darkly with a kind of bitter sadness while she expressed her thanks for the compliment.

Kleinpoppen and his mother went into the cottage for a bit of refreshment, but they didn't stay long. When they left, they walked past Alvin, who, having recovered his sense of himself, was loudly talking to a group of people Kleinpoppen didn't recognize.

"I remember the young men used to come around to see Nikki, and Pop would cross-examine them until they were sweating in their collars, ready to confess to any crime, performed or imagined..."

Eleanor Kleinpoppen took her son's arm as they walked back home. She looked as if she wanted to say something, probably something about her brother, but then she decided against it, and they walked home in silence, listening to the waves hit the shore, each lost in his and her own thoughts. Kleinpoppen devised a final verse for the Cleveland rock and roll song.

Baby, all the things you want to keep,
Baby, all the things you want to save.
You can't take them with you, babe.
They won't follow you to the grave.

Redemption

    Stan Reich awoke with the unpleasant knowledge that the day would not be relaxing. Shabbat. Saturday. A day of rest in any language. But not today. First, there was the service at the synagogue with the lame duck, Rabbi Shulman. Months before Stan and Leslie had agreed to attend the Saturday "learner's service," an instructional morning service in which the rabbi would explain the order and purpose of the liturgy. It had sounded interesting when he read the notice in the newsletter, and impulsively he'd signed the whole family up for it without considering that Lily's ballet recital was also scheduled for that morning. Then he really had to get a haircut that day. He was starting to feel unkempt, a feeling that grew on him with age even as his hair thinned, and next weekend was out since he'd be away at a teachers conference in Washington. And Tovah, his *zaftig* five-year-old girl, was going on her first sleepover that evening. It made him feel old.
    Stan rolled out of bed, careful not to wake Leslie. The cat, Shlomo, had just started his morning bleating out in the hallway, a din that could wake the dead if you didn't get to him quickly enough. Stan went down the stairs, shushing Shlomo, opened a can of low ash cat food, and spooned out a dish. Then he started the coffee. Not yet seven o'clock, he noticed, still time to read the morning paper in a leisurely way, at least. Wearing only a sweatshirt and his boxer shorts, Stan went out to the front porch to get the Baltimore *Sun*, sealed in a yellow plastic bag against the damp January weather. As he stepped back into the house, he caught sight of Leslie coming down the stairs, looking fatigued.

* * *

Rabbi Shulman was a bear of a man, lumbering, clumsy, furry, awkward. Heavy eyebrows, a beard that dripped off his face in black icicles. He had gout and walked gingerly with a stiff, upright carriage, like a man who had just shat in his pants. Since the Board had decided not to renew his contract, he had become increasingly withdrawn. Made slighting comments about the congregation, many of whose members were interfaith couples. He stood at the *bima*, looking out at the two dozen people in attendance.

"The Shabbat morning service is basically made up of five parts." Shulman rubbed his hands in the drafty, poorly heated sanctuary. Stan wished he'd kept his coat on like most of the others instead of hanging it up. "First, we have the warm-up prayers, the *birchot hashachar*, and the songs and psalms, *pesukai de-zimbra*. The sages knew you can't just come in off the street and be expected to focus on prayer, any more than an athlete can be expected to perform without doing warm-up exercises first. So the *siddur*, the prayerbook for the service, begins with these preliminary prayers. *Siddur* comes from the same root as *seder*, the Pesach feast. It means 'order.' So this is the order of the service.

"After the warm-up prayers, when we're all ready to begin praying in earnest, come the official morning prayers. First, we have the *Barechu*, the call to worship, when the rabbi calls all to prayer and the prayer service officially begins. The prayers concern Creation, Revelation—the giving of the Torah at Mount Sinai, the *Shema* and *Ve'ahavta*—and Redemption."

Ah, redemption! Stan thought, listening to Shulman drone on in his lofty, uninspired voice. Redemption. Old friend redemption. What exactly did it mean?

As if reading Stan's thoughts, Shulman went on, "...commemorating the exodus from Egypt, but redemption is the future, not the past. This order describes the course of history from creation, through revelation (which is the time we're living in now) to redemption and the messianic era, just as we do at the seder when we open the door for Elijah."

But what *was* redemption, Stan wondered vaguely. What did it look like and feel like? Sometimes the religious mumbo-jumbo was as confusing as the weathermen talking about "rain activity" and "thunderstorm events" or the traffic guys on the radio with their "accident working on the interstate." If redemption wasn't a metaphor, what was it? If it *was* a metaphor, what did it mean?

"Then we have the Amidah, community and individual prayers to God, including blessings in praise of God's devotion to our ancestors, to God's power and to God's name, the sanctification of Shabbat and the blessings in thanks to God for thanksgiving, prayer, and for peace. After the prayers comes the business portion of the service, the Torah reading and public business, the sermon, announcements and so on, before the service's concluding prayers, the *Aleinu* and *Mourner's Kaddish*. By the way, are there any questions? Please feel free to interrupt me with your questions. That's what this learner's service is supposed to be all about, after all."

Nobody spoke up or raised a hand.

"So, nobody has any questions. You understand it all. I guess this means I must be a good teacher. I've explained it all so clearly you haven't a single question." Shulman couldn't keep the sarcasm out of his voice. It was one of the things that had cost him his job.

Stan felt an impulse to raise his hand, to ask precisely what redemption *meant*. But he was afraid of sounding stupid and he canned it. He wasn't sure what *he* meant.

"Well, then, do we have a volunteer to lead us in responsively reading the 90th psalm?"

* * *

After the service there was a brief deli-style luncheon, bagels, lox, cream cheese, whitefish, but the Reiches had to leave quickly to get to the Ballet Academy on time for Lily's recital. Stan's mouth watered as he watched Mel Cohen set up the repast in the recreation room where he'd hung his coat.

"Any place I can put the soda to keep it cold?"

"Put it on the windowsill. That's a Bronx refrigerator," Shulman said, the New York accent flaring out for a moment from under the cultivated speculative Jewish Theological Seminary training.

* * *

"I don't see how they're going to get anybody better than Rabbi Shulman."

Leslie was one of Shulman's devoted followers. She liked his sermons and what he'd done for the children's religious school, providing texts and arranging field trips. He'd officiated at Tovah's naming ceremony.

"I don't know. Gary Grossman says they have a few candidates already," Stan replied.

"Who?"

Stan shrugged, keeping his eyes on the road. "There's a Reconstructionist lady from Philadelphia."

"If they pick a Reconstructionist, I'm quitting."

"There's also an Orthodox candidate who's never led a congregation before. A retired guy. He was a counselor in the Hillel at some university or other."

"Well, an Orthodox rabbi is better than a Reconstructionist one, at least. That's just officially sanctioned atheism."

"They think of themselves as a branch of Conservative Judaism, don't they?"

"I don't care what they consider themselves; they're atheists." Leslie yawned. "God I'm tired. I wish I could just take a nap."

A Better Tomorrow

* * *

"Point...plié...and point...and close," Miss Lisa, the ballet instructor, chanted in time to the *Nutcracker* coming from the CD player. "Point... plié...and point...and close. Keep your back straight, Samantha. All right. That's it. Point...plié...and point...and close."

Still not completely confident about the order of moves and still not very skilled, the children, all in blue leotards and pink tights, did their best to follow instructions. One of the children farted when they were all jumping in a circle, and they all tittered and gestured to deny responsibility. Miss Lisa tried to bring them back to attention.

The demonstration lasted an hour. Seeing the other dads with their video equipment, Stan wished he'd remembered to bring the Sony camcorder, even the Nikon point-and-shoot. In his preoccupation with the synagogue service, he'd completely forgotten. And here were all these memories eluding him forever. Kodak moments.

"Point...and flex...and out...and up...point...and flex... and out...and up...."

After it was over the parents applauded. Stan turned to Miss Lisa to thank her and congratulate her, and she unexpectedly hugged him. *Redemption*, Stan thought.

"Nice job, sweetie," Stan said to Lily, patting her on the head. "We're really proud of you."

"Let's take her to lunch," Leslie said. "She deserves it."

Stan glanced at his wristwatch reflexively. Was there time? But she did deserve to be rewarded. "Sure, okay."

"Let's go to Sutton Place. I have to buy a birthday present for Solomon at the toy store next door, anyway."

With quiet panic, Stan saw the day slipping away in these errands. But what else did he have to do?

"Solomon's what now? Three?" Leslie's sister Judy's son.

*   *   *

At last it was time to get his haircut. His barber closed at four on Saturdays, but when he got there a little before three, Stan found six people waiting ahead of him and both chairs occupied. The customer in John's chair was complaining about his cut, and Stan soon gathered he was the cause of the backlog.

"No, no!" he admonished the elderly barber. "The top is supposed to be the same length as the sides!"

A mere flicker of exasperation crossed John's face. He'd been at this for years; still, he seemed to be on a treadmill with this one.

"Let's try to even it up here, then. You want a brush cut?"

"Cut it any shorter and you'll need a one-way ticket for Parris Island!" Pat McClanahan said. A loud, red-haired man with a mustache, he was a fixture at the barbershop.

Carmela, the other barber, a woman who always made Stan think of Gertrude Stein, lost her patience. "Look, do you want it like this?" she said, holding out a framed photograph of her son, a marine.

"No, I don't want it cut *that* short, but I want it even all the way around."

"You're gonna get a one-way ticket to Parris Island, South Carolina!"

*   *   *

At ten to four Stan finally got into Carmela's chair. He preferred Carmela to John. She was faster, for one thing, more efficient. John snipped the air around your head as much as he clipped any actual hair. Carmela grabbed the hair between her fingers and snipped gently. McClanahan had gotten John's seat.

"Oh, man, John! I thought I'd never get into this seat when

Parris Island kept on fussing about his haircut! I never thought I'd make it! But here I am, finally. Like Father Clancy used to say, My Redeemer Liveth!" He burst out in a loud guffaw.

Redemption! Stan thought. As simple as sitting in a barber's chair.

"Don't forget to clip my eyebrows and the hair in my nose, would you, John?" McClanahan went on, and then he remembered something. "Damn, this morning I had an eyelash stuck in my eye. I couldn't get the damn thing out." He chuckled. "It was like the time I was sitting in my lounger, in my reclining chair. I was sitting there watching television, leaning back, and damn if something didn't land in my ear. Turned out it was a cockroach dropping from the ceiling, right into my ear. And I tried and tried but I couldn't get the damn thing out. Finally it crawled out of my ear after I'd gone to sleep."

Stan looked anxiously at the wall clock. Already after four. The mother of Tovah's friend, Frances, was stopping by the Reiches' soon to get Tovah for the sleepover. Stan wished passionately to be there when they arrived, to see the baby off. Not that Tovah would miss him that much if he weren't there, but the sleepover loomed in his mind as a milestone event, and he wanted to be there to see her go. Maybe redemption was getting *out* of the barber's chair.

"Boy, it goes with the territory." Clipping the hair over his ear, Carmela made eyes over at McClanahan.

"You don't believe him?"

"A bug in your ear would keep you awake. You couldn't go to sleep."

"The guy's a talker, that's for sure."

"Don't I know it."

Stan felt a jolt of gratification at this almost conspiratorial confidence. McClanahan blabbered on, unheeding.

"Yes sir, John! Damn if I could get that there bug out of my ear! But when it was gone, man! What a relief! Like father

Clancy used to say! My Redeemer Liveth!"

* * *

When he got home, Tovah had already gone. Frances' mom had come about half an hour earlier. Tovah was so excited, though, Leslie assured him, she hadn't missed him. *Late in arriving to a home where he wasn't even missed.* An epitaph. The summary of his life.

At dinner, it seemed like about half a dozen people were missing. They ate silently.

"I wonder what Shulman meant when he was talking about redemption," Stan said. "Some life after death fantasy where you're re-united with the people you've lost?"

"He didn't really say, did he?"

"You mean, he didn't really know?"

"Well, you heard him. He mentioned some beliefs Jews have about the longed-for messianic age, when everybody is righteous and freedom and justice reign."

Stan's heart sank. More religious mumbo-jumbo. "No, I mean, redemption from what?"

"Well, sin, I guess. Whatever the opposite of righteousness is."

"No, I mean—what does it feel like? To be redeemed?"

"Maybe it's just one of those ideals you strive to achieve, and maybe you get closer and closer to it but you don't ever attain it. You know what I mean?"

"Shulman didn't really say that, did he?"

"I wish the synagogue would reconsider their decision and renew his contract," Leslie lamented, changing the subject. "He's such a thoughtful man!"

"I find him a little arrogant," Stan said. "I'm glad we decided to get rid of him."

"You can call it arrogance if you want; it's just that he's so much more knowledgeable than anybody else."

"And he never lets you forget it, either."

"You didn't find the learner's service enlightening?"

"He never explained what redemption was."

"Yes, he did."

"Then what is it?"

"I thought it was boring," Lily interrupted in a sullen voice that was on the brink of whining.

Stan looked over at his daughter. Though she wouldn't admit it, she missed Tovah, too. He suddenly felt a great wave of pity for Lily.

"You did a really fine job in ballet today, Lily."

Leslie agreed. "We were so proud when Miss Lisa singled you out for line leader."

Then Stan had an idea. "Why don't we go to the movies tomorrow, the whole family?"

"Oh, yes! Can we?" Lily transformed from incipient grumpiness to hopeful glee right before Stan's eyes, suddenly so excited she jumped from her chair and looked pleadingly from one parent to the other, the way Shlomo did when he was hungry.

Leslie seemed to brighten at the idea, too. "We could pick Tovah up at Frances' house and go to lunch from there."

"Okay, then it's settled." Stan suddenly felt happy at the prospect of sitting huddled together in a darkened theater with his family, watching a movie.

After doing the dishes, they all went up to bed. Stan and Leslie tucked Lily in and then went to their bedroom. They made quiet love and then fell soundly asleep, snug in the expectation of the next day's pleasures. Leslie fell asleep first, and Stan drifted off later, lulled by an intimation of an elusive state of grace.

Mishpocheh

"Seems like I spent most of my weekends driving my kids from one place to another," Sidney Feit said to Robert Kleinpoppen. They had met by chance in the locker room at the Downtown Athletic Club where both were members. "Birthdays, Bar Mitzvahs, sleepovers. My Dad never took me nowhere. But you know what I did? I used to make my son read me the editorials in the paper while I drove. Figured I'd get some good out of it. And you know what? To this day that's the first thing he reads in the paper." Sidney chuckled at the memory. "I said to him, 'Mark, what's the first thing you read in the paper?' 'The editorial page!' he says like I'm meshuggah. 'Don't you remember? You always made me read them to you in the car!'"

"And you know what? He makes his kids do the same thing now!"

"Well, after the birthday party I have to pick Andy up in Reisterstown and bring him and Leah to the Purim Carnival at the shul."

"Rabbi Shulman's reading the Megillah?"

"I guess so. He's here until Shavuot, is my understanding."

"That's how long the contract goes."

"You coming?"

"To the Purim carnival? Nah. It's for kids." Feit shrugged awkwardly, pulling on his trousers.

"Shulman does a great Megillah interpretation."

"I've also got some family business to tend to," Sidney said, just vaguely enough not to invite questions. "*Mishpocheh*."

"Okay, well, I'll be seeing you." Feit was just buckling his belt when Kleinpoppen left the locker room.

Sally, one of Feit's grandchildren, just out of college—his son Mark's kid—was marrying a gentile. It was breaking Mrs. Feit's heart. Ellie regarded intermarriage as worse than death. Hitler's final victory, she called it, the extinction of the Jews. She had even sat *shivah* for Benny, her sister's son, when he married a Japanese girl.

But the latest development was that the boy, whose name was Brian, might convert, and the family was meeting at Mark's and Barbara's to discuss the pros and cons.

The whole business of conversion was troubling to Feit for the implications that eluded him. Who cared? So what? Beyond the ones who checked your pedigree, like hall monitors checking your pass. It was like the concept of "chosenness" that the goyim found so vexing. Feit almost never heard a Jew talk about it, but he was always being challenged by gentiles who suspiciously asked what it meant to be "chosen," as if they feared he thought he was "superior" to them. Not that he wanted to be part of a religion that went about trying to convert everybody to its beliefs, but if somebody wanted to join, why not?

Dressed, Feit went over to the soda machine and got a Gator Ade. Eighty-five cents, he noted, annoyed, when the machine spat back a nickel and dime, like a couple of constipated turds. He almost choked on his first sip; his eye caught the wall clock. He was fifteen minutes late for the family gathering.

* * *

"I was talking with Bob Kleinpoppen down at the club. He's going to the Megillah reading at the shul. You know he's a convert?"

"Bob Kleinpoppen? I knew there was something about him I didn't really feel comfortable with," Ellie said. She'd been fuming to her son and daughter-in-law because her husband was late—as he always was. Now she seemed to take it out on him. Whatever he said, she'd surely find fault with it.

"Kleinpoppen? He's okay. He does a good job with the newsletter."

"Newsletter schmoozletter."

"Well he does."

"Did I say he didn't?"

"What? You don't consider him Jewish?"

"Well, there are those who would say he's not."

"But what do you say?"

"What was his conversion? Reform? Conservative? It wasn't Orthodox. No way an Orthodox rabbi would convert him."

"Jenny Krupnick's a convert, too. Herman and Ruthie get more naches from her than they do from all their own kids put together."

"Jenny's one thing. Sally's pisher's another."

"Brian, but I thought we were talking about Bob Kleinpoppen."

"Whatever."

"I kind of feel sorry for the kid. Brian," Mark said, interposing between his parents. He knew how risky that was, like trying to separate two fighting cats. You could easily get hurt yourself.

"Well, I do, too, but only in the way you feel sorry for a nebbish. The drek and the chozzerai that kid eats. Sally told me. Bacon cheeseburgers, fried clams."

"We aren't completely kosher ourselves," Barbara said. "I say we give him a chance. He's willing to meet Sally halfway. He wants to convert."

"There's already enough tsuris to go around without looking for more," Feit agreed, looking at his wife. "Let's be open-minded about it."

Mark picked up a copy of the synagogue newsletter. "There's a seven-week workshop at Jewish Family Services for interfaith couples," he said, nodding toward the notice on one of the pages. "It's supposed to help couples understand their own and their partner's religion and ethnic background. There's also a one-shot deal called 'When a Child Intermarries.' It's for parents and grandparents." He looked significantly at his parents.

Sidney laughed, looking at his son holding the newsletter. "I was just telling Kleinpoppen about how I used to make you read me the editorials when I took you places in the car."

"What's it cost?" Ellie asked sharply, looking annoyed at her husband.

"There's a number to call for registration and fees," Mark said, and then he read from the article, "'Such topics as "Conversion to Judaism in Jewish Thought and History," "Raising Jewish Children" and "Roles of the Partner, Parents, In-Laws and Friends" are discussed, along with "The Conversion Process" and "Making Jewish Choices."'"

"Your friend Kleinpoppen sure is pushing this conversion bit in his newsletter," Ellie said to her husband, giving him her most ironic look. The look never failed to arouse her son.

"Are you going to stand in the way, Mom? I should have known."

"What? All I said was—"

"'Judaism welcomes sincere converts. In fact, Abraham, the founder of the Jewish people, was not born Jewish—'"

"Bob Kleinpoppen's writing that drek?"

"It's obviously from a press release."

"Who's conducting the course?" Ellie's voice had risen to a shrill pitch. It made Sidney remember the phrase he'd heard his southern friend Dave Price use down at the Athletic Club. She was so wound up it would take a dog to hear her fart.

"Rabbi Joel Cohen."

"A luftmentsh," Ellie snorted derisively.

"You've got it in for Reform rabbis, don't you, Eleanor?"

"What do you think?" Mark said. "You think Jesus would have been a Reform rabbi or Orthodox one?"

"Jesus! What are we bringing up Jesus for? Are *we* all going to convert and become Catholics or something to suit Sally?"

"Ellie! Can't you try to be more reasonable? You're always so hysterical!"

"It's a serious question," Mark said, his brown eyes gleaming with mischief. "Jesus was a Jew, after all. What was he up to? What was he badgering the other Jews about?"

"I won't stand for this!" Ellie cried, standing up. A dramatic gesture was imminent. It was inevitable. The pattern was so familiar to Sidney; he told himself he should have seen it coming. Ever since he was a boy Mark had needled his mother until she made some ultimate demonstration of her feelings. And nothing got accomplished.

And the family? The family went on. As usual.

"We could have gone to the Purim party instead," Sidney lamented, watching as Ellie left the room in a door-slamming huff and Mark, smiling like the Cheshire cat, innocently perused the newsletter. "We could have heard Rabbi Shulman read the Megillah."

One in Every Generation

Dear Congregation Member:

Recently, the Board of Directors has decided NOT to renew the contract of our Rabbi, Alan Shulman. The reason they have given is that the rabbi has resigned, but the fact is that this was not his decision. In other words, this group of ten people has decided not to offer a contract to the rabbi whom many of us have much respect for and whom we would like to see continue as our rabbi.

Please check one of the following statements and return this form to Leonard Finkelstein in the enclosed envelope.

___ I agree with the Board's decision not to renew Rabbi Shulman's contract.

___ I support Rabbi Shulman and would like to have him return as our spiritual leader.

Marvin Cohen was furious. An anonymous letter had been sent to all the members of the congregation questioning the Board's decision not to renew Rabbi Shulman's contract. The politically astute president of the synagogue had worked out the delicate maneuverings whereby the Board had accepted the rabbi's resignation, thereby putting a good face for everybody on the firing, and now here was this letter, upsetting everything. Rumor had it the *Jewish Times* had a copy and were going to run a story about it. Not only this, but some Iago had whispered to Marvin that Shulman had sanctioned the letter.

A week and a half before Passover, Marvin called an emergency meeting of the Board of Directors to discuss the events and what sort of response he should make, if any. The meeting lasted two hours, and it was not clear to Robert Kleinpoppen what decision had been made. Marvin had asked him to attend for reasons that were still unclear to Kleinpoppen. Perhaps, as editor of the synagogue newsletter, his duty was to provide editorial direction if a written response were required. Or maybe Marvin saw Kleinpoppen as his spin doctor, the Goebbels to his Hitler, if such an analogy were not inappropriate to officials of a synagogue.

The Board hastily met in the basement of the synagogue, still set up from the Sunday School pot luck supper the evening before, row after row of folding tables with ten folding metal chairs per table.

"The reason I've asked you to come this evening," Marvin ponderously intoned, "is to discuss the anonymous letter that's been sent by somebody to the rest of the congregation." Marvin was a tall, sandy-haired lawyer with large hazel eyes that continuously roved the room like a pair of watchdogs on the prowl. A bushy brown mustache seemed to emphasize the rubbery quality of his saliva-slick lips, and Kleinpoppen always found himself mesmerized by them, repelled but fascinated by their similarity to a couple of nightcrawlers, and he always lost track of what Marvin was saying.

"Leonard Finkelstein!" Gail Heyman interrupted with shrill insistence. She was a lawyer, too. Almost all of them were lawyers, Kleinpoppen reflected, full of crafty strategies to prevent or pursue lawsuits, quick with legal and judicial metaphors like "taking the stand," "cross-examining the witness," and "hung jury." Kleinpoppen counted them. Out of the nine people present, six of them were attorneys—Marvin, Gail, Harold Stern, Ben Rosen, Nathan Goodman, Alex Katz. Only he, Arlen Fox and Miriam Cantor were not in the legal profession.

"No," Marvin said. "I called Leonard and he said he had nothing to do with writing the letter. He'd only agreed to receive the responses. *After* Shulman had okayed the letter."

"He's a liar!"

"Can we just fire him?" Harold Stern asked Marvin. "Can't we just pay him the balance of his contract and tell him not to come back?"

"We don't have any evidence. This is just what Leonard told me."

"What's the big deal?" Arlen Fox said, looking flustered at Gail and Harold. "Shulman's just hanging himself. Let him cut his own rope. Everybody I've talked to thinks he's making an ass out of himself. They think he's being ridiculous." Arlen was a retired Physics professor. Easygoing, grayheaded and grandfatherly, with a gentle, boyish face, he liked to put a folksy spin on problems in an attempt to humanize and defuse them. This was not the OJ Simpson murder trial, after all.

"We could lose credibility with the rest of the Jewish community," Gail declared. "This is not just a tempest in a teapot. It could affect our future as a synagogue."

"Any truth to the rumor the *Jewish Times* is running a story?" Alex Katz asked. Alex wore half moon eyeglasses and fixed you with a stare over the tops of the semicircles. Probably a courtroom trick, Kleinpoppen guessed.

"I keep getting calls from them that I don't answer," Marvin said. "At first I just said it was old news. We accepted Shulman's resignation months ago. But then they started asking questions about the survey and I've stopped talking to them. Ted Wiener knows somebody at the Times and got it on the q.t. that they've got a story but they're sitting on it."

"That bastard!" Gail cried. Her dislike of Rabbi Shulman went back to his refusal to perform the wedding ceremony when her sister married a Catholic man who refused to convert.

"Well he's only making himself look foolish," Arlen repeated.

"Nevertheless, I ought to do something about it. What? Write a response to everybody? We can't just ignore it. People are expecting something."

"Which people?" Arlen said. "The only people I've talked to think he's making a fool of himself. They think he's losing credibility if anything."

"Besides, Marv," Harold said. "It's an *anonymous* letter. We don't even have to dignify it with a response. Responding to it gives it an integrity and a plausibility it doesn't have."

"So you don't think we should respond to the anonymous letter either?" Arlen asked Harold.

"Why should we? If they don't have the guts to sign it—"

"Nevertheless," Marvin said, raising his voice to command attention. "Nevertheless, we live in the real world, and somebody has sent this letter."

"There's always one in every generation, I mean congregation," Nathan Goodman said.

"I think you *should* write a response," Gail said. "Boards of Directors always suffer from a PR problem. Either they think we're the faceless party insiders of the politburo or they think we're jack-booted thugs."

"Okay, I move we write a personal letter to every member of the congregation denouncing the anonymous letter," Miriam Cantor said. A comely woman in her early forties, Miriam plainly wanted to get the meeting over with, probably had something else already planned for the evening.

"Second."

"Okay," Marvin said. "We have a motion on the table to write a response to the congregation, and Gail's seconded the motion. All those in favor—"

"Wait," Harold said. "What's this letter going to say?"

"I don't see why we have to react to everything Shulman does," Ben Rosen said. A small, dark, ferret-faced man who emphasized his diminutiveness by slouching down in his chair, he spoke in a petulant whine, like a boy at a table who was being made to eat something he didn't like. "Shulman's pulling the strings here. We're like his puppets. Why don't we just ignore this."

"Well, we don't want to get too defensive," Miriam said. "We don't want the letter to sound like we're apologizing or backtracking."

"Yes," Gail said, "Let's just keep it short and to the point."

"Emphasize that the letter did not come from the Board."

"An *anonymous* letter," Harold said.

Arlen looked at Harold. "I thought you opposed writing a letter."

"I'm just pointing out that the letter was anonymous."

"All right, but we've got a motion before us," Marvin said. Marvin was taking it all personally, like a private war with the rabbi.

"I withdraw the motion," Miriam said. "Maybe we should consider some other response. I can see how we might be falling into a trap by sending a letter. It kind of legitimizes the survey, Harold's right." Miriam glanced fleetingly at her wristwatch, a look of dismay dragging at her eyes.

"Well then what should we do?"

* * *

Kleinpoppen left the two-hour meeting not sure what conclusion the Board had come to; a number of motions had been made and withdrawn or defeated. Everybody wanted Shulman's ass in a sling, but nobody was sure how to get it there. Gail Heyman was the shrillest; she made Kleinpoppen think of a predatory bird. Her facial features were sharp and pointy, and her fingernails were painted red talons.

Only Miriam Cantor had been preoccupied with other matters. At one point, while the others haggled over the language of the not-as-yet agreed upon response to the anonymous letter, she had tugged back the sleeve of her blouse to glance at her wristwatch, and a pellet-shaped OB tampon had come flying out of her sleeve; she'd evidently concealed it there for emergency use. It landed on the dining table in front of Kleinpoppen. The Lone Ranger's silver bullet. Kleinpoppen discreetly pretended not to notice it. He wondered how he might return it to Miriam without bringing undue attention to the transaction. *Excuse me, Miriam, didn't I see this come flying out of your sleeve?* Everybody else must have seen it, too, unless they were so involved in the discussion that a tampon flying by did not phase them. Miriam reached her hand over in a lightening-quick gesture to retrieve the tampon, her hand moving so quickly it made Kleinpoppen think of quick-lidded frogs licking invisible insects out of the air. In any case, his attention was shot as far as the rest of the meeting went, and when they finally adjourned he felt too self-conscious to ask what decision they'd made.

Two days later, Kleinpoppen received Marvin's monthly column in the mail when he got home from work. *Chaverim* was a ten-page, two-column newsletter on 8-1/2" x 11" paper. In the left-hand column on page one, there was always a "Message from Our Rabbi," and in the adjacent front-page column, a "Message from Our President."

Marvin's column made Kleinpoppen catch his breath. It began: "*Chaverim*—Friends: Friends don't send friends unsigned letters..." He went on to imply that certain responsible people who should know better had a certain complicity in the composition and distribution of the letter; it was clear whom he meant. Kleinpoppen was not sure if he should publish it; it was sure to create bad feelings, and if the *Jewish Times* was having second thoughts about writing a news story about the affair, this would certainly resolve those doubts.

He did not want to tell Judy about the column because she was a Shulman supporter and it would be difficult to live with her. On the other hand, he had to talk to somebody. But he decided to wait until the morning. But in the morning when Kleinpoppen and his wife had their morning mug of coffee, he didn't really feel like talking about it, either. Only briefly, as

she was going out the door to her car, did he casually mention Marvin's column.
"Well, Marvin sure lets him have it in his monthly column."
"Lets who have it? The rabbi?"
"Well, it's not Arafat or Ariel Sharon."
"That creep! And you're going to let him get away with it? After you asked Edith Naden not to write a letter of protest to the editor?"
"Maybe Edith Naden wrote the anonymous letter."
"I'm late. Tell me about it later."

* * *

When Kleinpoppen got to work, his boss, Romanchuk, gave him the Rabbi's monthly column, which had just come over the fax machine.
"What is this 'From Our Rabbi' shit? Sounds like he's pissed off at somebody."
"Oh, it's just the monthly message from the rabbi for the synagogue newsletter I edit. They're getting rid of him."
"Who? The synagogue? You can do that? You can fire a rabbi?"
"Well, it's not like a Pope appoints him to be the parish priest or something. He's the spiritual leader, but he's also an employee. It's a fine line to tread. It requires political skills he didn't have."
"And you're firing him? You Jews are heartless sons of bitches." Romanchuk liked to needle Kleinpoppen with these little anti-semitic remarks; both knew he'd done much more ruthless things in his own business. Kleinpoppen shrugged and walked back to his cubicle with the fax.
"All the other congregations with which I have been affiliated have required those in positions of top leadership to attend services regularly," Shulman began his column.
"Any community is weakened when its leadership is largely

absent from the main activity of the institution, which in this case is prayer services. Leaders are expected to be both accessible to members and examples of involvement and commitment."

So now Shulman had thrown down the gauntlet, too. Kleinpoppen wondered if he ought to act like a referee or something, send both fighters back to their corners. But what could he do?

* * *

That night in bed, after Andy and Leah were asleep, Kleinpoppen turned to his wife.

"Well, Shulman gives as good as he gets."

"Oh yeah? What's he say?"

"He was complaining about 'the leadership' of the congregation not coming to services."

"Well, I think that's valid."

"Sure, publicly humiliate Marvin Cohen under the guise of righteousness."

"What did Marvin say in his column?"

"He was sniping at the writer of the anonymous letter; you could tell he thought Shulman wrote it. He also said the rabbi search was still going on and he hoped when we got a new rabbi that more members would come to services more regularly, a subtle implication that Shulman's a bore and an idiot."

"The *Jewish Times* will certainly have something to say now."

"Oh, the *Jewish Times*! Why is everybody so scared of the *Jewish Times*? Besides, who was it that said *any* publicity is good publicity?"

"Well, it wasn't OJ Simpson. You're going to print this stuff? It *does* make us look bad, petty and spiteful. Especially at this time of year, with Pesach almost here, it's unfortunate.

Why do they have to do this? Why do they have to try to annihilate each other? Jews have already got any number of people who'd gladly do it for them."

Kleinpoppen remembered Nathan Goodman's slip of the tongue at the board meeting. "Well, you know what the Haggadah says, there's one in every generation that rises up to destroy the Jews." But secretly, he had to admit, he was enjoying the excitement. Nothing like a bloodbath to liven things up.

The Shikker Rabbi

Let me say at the outset that I am not a particularly judgmental person; I do not hold people to strict standards of behavior, evaluate every action or deed as it reflects on the essential moral character of the actor, the doer. The Ten Commandments are good enough for me, though to tell you the truth I probably don't know them all, certainly can't recite them in order; I'm no expert on them except to say that they forbid killing and messing around with another person's spouse and property, and in general that covers everything. The lawyers can handle the details. I do appreciate a certain level of decorum, but I am not about to condemn anybody for a minor breach of the conventions.

Neither am I a very observant Jew. My father converted to Judaism to marry a woman whose family required it of him, and I was raised as a Jew and even went through my bar mitzvah. But after that my observance relaxed, and to tell the truth, in the regular course of the year, I only attend synagogue during the High Holidays and then only for as brief a visit as possible; I am not alone in this, of course. It's been years since I fasted on Yom Kippur, though I do feel a kind of reflexive guilt when I drink a glass of water or eat an apple on that day of repentance. An incorrigible sneak. But if there *is* a God, I'm sure It will overlook such a minor detail.

I married a Jewish girl, much to my mother's relief and my father's indifference. (My mother wept privately but bitterly when my older sister Judy married an Indonesian fellow, but my father welcomed Dewi and Rachael into the family with equal warmth). Until our first daughter reached the age of two, however, we did not belong to a synagogue. My parents are

Conservative Jews, but Rachael and I tended toward Reform. We finally joined a new congregation that had formed in our eclectic city neighborhood, a mongrel community that boasts a Baptist, a Presbyterian and an Episcopal church as well as a mosque. We do not live in one of the predominantly Jewish suburbs where temples as vast as college campuses thrive with congregations numbering in the tens of thousands. We told ourselves that we liked the idea of actually helping to determine the philosophical outlook of our shul, and that the people all seemed friendly, sincere and intelligent, but I suspect the convenience made the final difference when we decided to join.

My wife even helped select the new rabbi when the original one decided to retire. She attended a few meetings to review credentials, that is, though I think it was the president of the congregation, Marvin Cohen, who finally extended the offer to Alan Shulman, a single man in his thirties from somewhere in Long Island.

Rabbi Shulman joined just before the High Holidays several years ago. Several rabbis were in attendance at the services, including old Mordechai Bloom, the crusty old guy who would soon be retiring. Rabbi Bloom spoke in a deep rumbling voice with only the barest trace of Eastern Europe discernable in its volcanic resonance. He wore his voluminous floor-length tallis as if it were an academic gown at a college commencement. I almost expected him to hand out diplomas while he strolled solemnly around the *bima* rumbling on and on about renewal of faith, obedience to God and responsibility to the community.

* * *

Sober-faced, almost mournful, with a drooping dark moustache that made him look even sadder, Rabbi Shulman debuted at the first Rosh Hashanah service in the role of chazan. He had a remarkable voice and could have been the cantor by profession. His voice hit all of the highs and most of the lows, as full-bodied as a tenor in a black Baptist church on a Sunday morning, as haunting as a muezzin yodeling out the call to evening prayer. The kind of voice you might hear at Carnegie Hall or the Metropolitan Opera. Everybody was impressed. And though I did not attend, opting instead to take my daughter Leah home and there wolfing down an egg salad sandwich and reading the box scores in the American League East pennant race, Rachael told me Rabbi Shulman sparkled with wit and wisdom during the discussion of Abraham's near-sacrifice of Isaac that followed the morning service.

The only reason we attended the second Passover seder at Beth Chaim at all was that our second daughter, Lisa, was born in January and we had her naming ceremony in mid-March, sponsoring a kiddush in the basement rec room afterwards. Marv Cohen sidled up next to me with a cup of Manischewitz Concord Grape while I nibbled at a slice of challah and suggested we might like to come. In a convivial rush of good feeling not untinged with a sense of guilt, I agreed.

These people are always calling us up and informing us about guest speakers and Friday night dinners and special events that we really *should* attend and that they would just *love* to see us at. Ellie Goodman, an officer of some sort in the congregation bureaucracy, is the person assigned to hounding us, and when we do make it to one of these events—we took Leah to a Chanukkah party in December—she chides me with a line like, "We so rarely get a chance to *see* you!" In fact, moments before Marv cornered me at the kiddush, Ellie had expressed her deep regret that we had been unable to bring Leah to the Purim celebration in February. I made up some lame story about a household stricken with flu.

Prior to the kiddush, during the morning service, I had been impressed by Rabbi Shulman's unorthodox sense of humor. The naming ceremony took place within the context of the regular Shabbat morning service. "Marvin Cohen has asked me to remind you that annual membership dues should have been paid by now," he announced at the beginning of the service, and then: "I'm reminded of the story about the boy who came to the shul during the High Holiday services without a ticket." Shulman smiled enigmatically to himself and then went on. "He told the usher he *had* to see his father, and when the usher told the boy he could not enter the shul without a ticket, the boy insisted that the matter was urgent. 'All right,' the usher said at last, 'but you'd better not let me catch you davaning!'"

Nervous laughter followed the joke. The congregation was not certain what he was getting at. Did he mean to insult President Cohen? Kindly Marv. Everybody was protective of the affable, good-hearted, though slightly bumbling Marvin Cohen, Mister Diplomatic. Marv was like Everybody's Dad. But Shulman, smiling urbanely, moved on to the rest of the service without further comment, and the joke was forgotten.

Still, it was no wonder that Shulman's contract was not being extended beyond that year. There had been a minor controversy about this among his faithful followers, and a letter of protest polling the congregation on his dismissal was sent, though nothing ever came of it except an indignant newsletter article by Marvin. Shulman was already on his way out even before the Passover seder fiasco.

Rachael had reserved the second and third aliyot for us; she took the second, being a Levi, and I said the third blessing over the Torah, after which Lisa's naming took place. Lisa's Hebrew name is Aliza Chava; she is named, Ashkenazi-style, after recently deceased relatives, Rachael's grandfather Louis and my mother's uncle Chaim, a venerable old guy who had died the year before at the age of 106.

But during the naming ceremony Rabbi Shulman kept referring to our older daughter Leah as "Sheila." I admit, the names Leah, Lisa and Sheila have a similar sound, and some confusion might inevitably occur, but both Rachael and I tried subtly to correct the rabbi. When he said, "Lisa joins her older sister Sheila in the community," Rachael pointedly said in a loud whisper to our daughter, "Come over here, Leah." She had strayed away from the *bima* though not that far away. My wife's intention was pretty obvious. I chimed in, "Leah, come over here. The rabbi is talking about you and Lisa, Leah."

"Sheila, you are fortunate to have a sister and parents like Lisa, Mark and Rachael," Shulman said, insisting on the wrong name, as if the ceremony were really all about re-naming our first daughter. Leah picked up on it immediately.

"Daddy, he called me Sheila," she said. The congregation tittered. There were only about two dozen people there for the morning service, a bare minyan if you were only counting the men.

"Sheila, stand there by your mother," Rabbi Shulman said, oblivious to Leah's complaint, and he resumed the ceremony. It was oddly unsettling, but I mention these incidents mainly because they foreshadow the disaster at the Passover seder.

* * *

The second seder began at five o'clock on Thursday evening, to accomodate those who would be going to work the next day. We had spent the first seder the previous evening with Rachael's brother's family. Traditionally, the first seder involves only the family while the second involves a larger circle of the community. The basement rec room of Beth Chaim was filled with about a dozen folding tables, each of which was set with ten places. When we arrived, we were pleased to find that we shared a table with David and Bonnie Reich, a couple around our age with two young sons about the same age as our girls. The Reichs were pretty deeply involved in the congregation; David organized sports events and coached teams for kids, and Bonnie wrote the religious school news for the newsletter, *Chaverim*. David's parents from New Jersey and his brother Sheldon from Los Angeles were there as their guests. The brother was rather effeminate, and throughout the evening seemed to be dodging his father's inquiries into his private life, from what I occasionally overheard. (I could have sworn Mister Reich used the Yiddish word "feigele" several times. Faggot). David, meanwhile, ducked out before the seder got underway. Bonnie apologized for him, explaining that he had gone home to take care of the baby, who was rather fussy that evening, but I suspected that he had bailed out to watch the Orioles game on television. All at once I felt a little marooned. The parents from New Jersey were plainly uninterested in Rachael and me; they spoke Yiddish to each other and to their children, though I don't know how much of it Sheldon or Bonnie understood. So we sat there tending to Leah and Lisa, waiting for the festivities to begin. There was a room at the back for small children, but Leah preferred to stay with us.

The seder did not get underway at five o'clock as planned. Rabbi Shulman had not arrived, and we had to wait for him before we started. Marvin Cohen and his wife, Ruthie, sat at a separate table up front facing the rest of us, the table where Rabbi Shulman was also supposed to sit and preside over the seder. Together, red-faced, overweight and smiling selfconsciously, Marv and Ruthie made me think of a benevolent television Mom and Dad. Finally, just after six, the congregation having become rather restless, Marvin began the seder even though Rabbi Shulman had not arrived.

Ellie Goodman had called a few days before to ask Rachael and me if we would participate by reading, in Hebrew and in English, part of the Haggadah text explaining the Passover symbols. Everybody had a part. So after the first of the four cups of wine and the washing of the hands, which Marv and Ruthie did for all of us, sparing the congregation the hassle, a succession of small children got up before the assembled guests and chanted the four questions through the cheap makeshift microphone that squealed with electronic feedback like a banshee. Harold and Sharon Baumgartner began the text about how you explain the meaning of Pesach to the four sons, reading about the intelligent son; Irving and Susan Brookmeyer, Alex and Marcia Katz, Ed and Judith Fogel finished them up, the ill-mannered, the indifferent, and the incompetent sons. A succession of others read about the suffering, sorrow and triumph of the Jews in Egypt. We counted out the ten plagues with drops of wine, and everybody joined in a spirited rendition of Dayenu. Three more couples got up to read about the three Passover symbols, including Rachael and me. We read the explanation of *maror*—the bitter herbs. Finally, after the second cup of wine and the ritual washing of the hands (this time everybody washed hands), we broke for the meal.

"*Es gezunte heit!*" Mrs. Reich said to Sheldon. Eat well. Enjoy your meal.

* * *

Rabbi Shulman finally arrived as we were eating the matzoh ball soup. He did not come in with an apologetic smile, an excuse, even a shrug of the shoulders. He did not come in like a politician, shaking hands and touching arms and kissing the women. Nor was he philosophical, solemn, aloof. He swaggered in, a little off-balance, like a pirate on a rolling deck in high seas, took his place next to Ruthie Cohen, opened his Haggadah and began to hum "Dayenu," as if there were nothing unusual about his late appearance.

"Look, Rabbi Shulman finally made it," Bonnie Reich said to her mother-in-law.

"That's the rabbi?" Sheldon asked. "He looks more like a concentration camp survivor." He smiled rakishly at his irreverence.

"Sheldon!" Mrs. Reich scolded, glancing briefly at Rachael and me to see if we had been shocked.

"Only, he doesn't look like he's surviving all that well!"

"Such *chutzpah*," Mr. Reich chuckled.

Rachael spoke up then to relieve the Reichs from any embarrassing family scene. "I wonder why he was late."

I shrugged. "Maybe traffic was heavy. Where does he live? Silver Spring?"

We all glanced at Rabbi Shulman as he leaned into Ruthie Cohen's bosom, confiding something to Marv and his wife. The shocked, worried look on Ruthie's face said that something was wrong. We could only guess what it was, but once the reading of the Haggadah resumed, it became apparent what was the matter.

After the pound cake and the macaroons, Rabbi Shulman tinkled on his glass with a spoon to get everybody's attention. Amplified by the cheap, echoing microphone, it had the shrill reverberation of a doorbell gone haywire.

"People," Rabbi Shulman said. "People. People." Even after the room was silent he tapped the glass several more times and repeated the word. The fuzzy microphone picked it all up and hurled it back into our faces, ten times as big as life. In a momentary flash of insight that immediately became muddled in doubt, I saw he was trying to clear his mind, to marshal his fragmented thoughts. But then without warning he began to chant a psalm in Hebrew, and it was as if nobody but he were in the room. People began to look at one another dubiously and then to roll their eyes.

Sensing the restlessness and confusion, Shulman, hunched over the table so that his shoulders formed a sort of shell, peered up under his brows at the congregation and stared for a long moment before saying harshly, "The Lord provides, my friends. The Lord provides."

Again there was a flurry of whispered exchanges and meaningful looks before the rabbi directed us to fill our cups for the third time. Then he resumed his private mumbling. Marvin and Ruthie looked embarrassed and tried to smile reassuringly around the room. I noticed Ellie Goodman in her seat at one of the dining tables shaking her head in disbelief.

At our table, Bonnie Reich leaned toward her mother-in-law. "I guess the rabbi's in his cups tonight."

"A *shikker*," Mrs. Reich said, disgusted. "*Ver volt dos geglaibt?*" Who would have believed it.

Although we had poured the third cup of wine, Rabbi Shulman never actually commanded us to drink it, and before long we were already extending our hospitality to Elijah, part of the ritual of the fourth cup. We all sipped and slurped up our third cup as we could while Shulman instructed Ruthie to open the door for the beloved prophet Elijah. I may have been mistaken, but I thought I saw Shulman briefly pat Ruthie's ass when she stood up to open the door. I looked around at the others at my table, but nobody registered the level of outrage I would have expected. In any case, our attention was soon distracted by Shulman, standing to his feet with Elijah's cup of wine in his hand and thundering, "Elijah, this Bud's for you!"

There were a few titters in the audience, but by this time everybody was numbed into a sort of shocked silence.

About then Leah began to whine. She had been a patient little girl for several hours now, and she seemed to sense the discomfort of everybody around her. In any case, I found it convenient to take her to the children's room and thus escape the oppressive seder.

When I finally returned, a few of the older men in the congregation were making no disguise of their indignation, sitting in their seats and glaring at the rabbi, while he continued to mumble on, singing the praises of God in English and in Hebrew.

At last Shulman looked up and said, "These endless words of praise to God after the meal always remind me of the Yom Kippur story where the rabbi is beating his breast in front of the whole congregation, bewailing himself as a sinner, as a worthless soul before the Almighty One Blessed Be He. When he's done, the cantor does the same, weeping and moaning and confessing his worthlessness to the All Powerful. 'I am nothing, nothing, nothing, O Lord!' he cries.

"Then the poorest member of the congregation, the schlemiel who sweeps out the shul on every day but the Sabbath, a lowly, humble, shamefaced little man, so moved by the rabbi and the cantor, stands up and *he* starts to weep and beat his breast and exclaim to the Almighty, 'I am nothing! Oh, forgive me, Lord, for I am but a helpless sinner! I am nothing!'

"Then the cantor turns to the rabbi and says, 'Look who thinks *he's* nothing!'"

When nobody laughed at the joke, Shulman, still hunched over like a creature with an enormous burden on his back and peering up from under his eyebrows like the Cheshire cat, said, "And then there's the one about the gay rabbi who blew his shofar. But seriously, folks—!"

"I've had about enough of this," Sheldon Reich said, seething with indignation, and he got up from our table and left the room.

At that point, Rabbi Shulman stood up, grabbed the microphone like a nightclub entertainer, and began to croon:

"Let's go to the shul!
Let's go to the shul!
You can listen to the chazan,
You can see the rabbi davan
At the shul!
Let's go to the shul (oh baby)
Let's go to the shul (oh baby)
Yeah, oh, yeah
To the shul!"

Marvin Cohen stood up from his table and gawked at Shulman like a country rube at a city skyscraper, mouth open, eyes glazed with wonder. He grabbed the nearest Haggadah from the table and began to read aloud the concluding prayer, a makeshift tactic, pis aller, at the end shouting above Shulman to drown him out:

"*L'Shanah habaah b'Yerushalayim*! Next year in Jerusalem!"

After that, everybody left hurriedly. Shulman continued to shuffle around with the microphone in his hand, seemingly unaware of the confusion and disarray in the shul. Rachael and I bundled Leah and Lisa into their coats and headed for our car.

"*Ich fil zich opgenart*," Mr. Reich said ahead of us, enraged. If he felt like the rabbi made a fool out of *him*, imagine how Marv and Ruthie Cohen must have felt.

A few weeks later, a letter came in the mail postmarked Las Vegas, Nevada. It was from Rabbi Shulman, apologizing for his behavior. "I hope you will except my sincere apology," he wrote, and I wondered if he had misspelled the word on purpose. "Without going into detail, my difficulty that evening originated from a medical alert." Again I wondered at the phrasing. What did he mean by a medical "alert"?

While I pondered over the letter, the telephone rang. It was Ellie Goodman calling to tell us about the wonderful Friday night service that was coming up and to ask if we wanted to make reservations for dinner. I said I would have to talk to Rachael about it, though I had an idea we were supposed to go out of town that weekend.

"By the way, we just got an interesting letter from Rabbi Shulman."

"I know. We got the same one."

"So he's no longer the rabbi?"

"It was just so embarrassing. Marvin asked him to resign the next day."

"That's a shame."

"Yes, it is. Sometimes he had such wonderful ideas and insights."

"He seemed very witty."

"A first-rate Torah scholar."

"This is the only time it's happened?"

"No, he got pie-eyed on one other occasion, too. Twice was

just too many times. It's such a shame."

"It really is too bad. So he's moved out west?"

"The rumor is he's got a nightclub act," Ellie confided. "Singing and playing the piano."

"Well, he did have a wonderful voice." I smiled at the memory of his takeoff on "Let's Go to the Hop."

"He could have been a cantor." Ellie sighed heavily, lamenting the loss.

"Well, I'll talk to Rachael about Friday night, Ellie. Thanks for calling."

"Such a shame," Ellie continued, as if she hadn't heard me. "A drunk. All his brilliant ideas and that beautiful voice gone to waste. A drunk. A *shikker* rabbi."

Just Say Yes

"You're Jewish?" Richard Potash's voice carries a tone of curiosity and disbelief. He evidently hadn't assumed such. Potash himself has New York Jew written all over him, from his prominent nose to his sharp brown eyes to his wiseguy accent. Even his beard, gray and clipped close to the skin, accenting the cheekbones, proclaims him a Jew. Doctor Freud of Vienna. Lanky, Potash is the kind of guy who looks good in turtlenecks, corduroys and tennis shoes, sporty and youthful, even in his mid-sixties.

"Well, I converted," Morgenbesser begins to explain, and Potash interrupts.

"So you're Jewish, then."

"Well, it was a Conservative conversion, and I guess there are those in Israel who wouldn't recognize it."

"Fuck 'em," Potash says. "You're Jewish. You converted. Period. You'll never satisfy everybody."

They sit quietly in the dim steamroom, towels wrapped about their waists, listening to the hiss from the jet. It's a Tuesday morning; they're the only ones here. Morgenbesser has taken the day off from his job with an enormous federal agency, and Potash, a semi-retired photographer, routinely chooses these quiet times to come to the gym, swim and sit in the steamroom.

"I never really cared much for the religion," Potash offers after a minute, breaking the silence. "But I do like Passover. The Seders. I like the company."

Morgenbesser converted to Judaism a decade and a half earlier. What prompts his reticence in the steamroom is an encounter he's just had with Ellen Herxheimer out on the exercise bikes. Ellen is a social worker with a bubbly personality that invites confidence. Morgenbesser finds himself spilling to her whenever they meet. He'd just been telling her about his daughter's forthcoming bat mitzvah ceremony.

"You don't look Jewish to me," Ellen exclaims, ingenuous, in that chatty, gossipy voice, and Morgenbesser admits that he's a convert. It feels like a confession, too, as if he were owning up to a shameful secret and coming up short in her estimate.

"I didn't think so," Ellen chirps. She does not hold it against him; she does not think he is a fraud. "I don't know. I guess I just don't think of Jews as a religion so much, you know? I think of Jews in terms of eth*nicity*." She makes it sound exotic, sexy. "Like Italians. Warm, always talking, fun to be around."

Morgenbesser is the first to admit he isn't a really dynamic personality, but somehow he gets the impression that Ellen is telling him he just doesn't belong to the club; he's just not funny or provocative enough.

"Why'd you do it?"

"Convert? Oh, it's kind of complicated." Sometimes Morgenbesser feels as though people are trying to get to the flight data recorder in the center of his soul to unravel the mystery of the plane wreck that is his personality. "Basically my wife asked me to, before we were married."

"Yeah, a lot of my Jewish clients are in the same situation. Either they're involved with somebody who's not Jewish and their parents disapprove, or they feel guilty about it themselves, or—"

"Do you recommend conversion to them?"

"I let them work out their own solutions. Anyway, so your daughter's having a bat mitzvah, huh? That's very exciting! I remember when my daughter became a bat mitzvah..."

"Your daughter's having her bas mitzvah, huh?" Potash says, speaking in the old-fashioned Ashkenazaic way in which the Hebrew t's are Yiddish s's. He seems unimpressed by the rite of passage. His tone says he could give a shit. Morgenbesser tried the news out on him, partly just to say something, but also he wants to compare the response with Ellen's. "Is she excited?"

"A little nervous. Afraid she'll fuck up in front of the congregation when she chants her Torah portion."

Potash chuckles. "I went through that when I was a kid. Of course, girls didn't do it when I was growing up, just the boys." Morgenbesser wonders if this is simply age talking or if it's "authentic Jew" talking to "Moses-come-lately." How things used to be before the Jews became Protestants and let the goyim in. "Haven't been back in a synagogue since."

Nah, file that away under "Paranoia." Potash just doesn't go in for religious ceremonies. In fact, he stands up now and excuses himself. As the steam starts to hiss again from the valve, Morgenbesser is pretty sure he's uncomfortable with the subject of religion and his departure is in the nature of flight.

* * *

"Busy today?"

Morgenbesser looks up from the computer screen. Bessie, one of the cleaning people, stands at the entrance to his cubicle, dustmop in hand and cleaning cart behind her.

"Oh, hi. Well, it's steady. Always something to do."

Bessie fusses around the small cubicle, sweeping crumbs off the floor and dusting the file cabinet. She glances at the framed photographs of his children on his desk, already several years out of date.

"Girls excited about Christmas?"

It's always a tough one for Morgenbesser. This time he decides to level with her.

"Chanukah. Yes, they're excited about Chanukah."

"What you say? Hanookee?"

"That's right. Chanukah. We're Jewish."

"You all don't celebrate Christmas?" It seems inconceivable to her, and Morgenbesser tries to relieve her distress.

"No, but there's Chanukah. It's the same thing." He knows he's made a mistake. He has some explaining to do, and he would just rather go back to work.

"You all give each other presents?"

"Yes."

"You all have a tree and everything?"

"No, but we light candles. It's called 'the festival of lights.'"

Bessie shakes her head. "No, it ain't the same thing without a tree."

"I don't know. We give presents and stuff. It seems like pretty much the same thing."

Bessie looks skeptical as she shuffles out of Morgenbesser's cubicle, and he feels as if he's ruined her day in some ineffable way.

* * *

"Mister Morgenbesser, did you take your wife's name when you got married?" Stephanie Roth, an insouciant mother of five in the English 101 class Morgenbesser teaches in the evening at a local community college, begins class by putting him on the spot. In the context of an essay assignment he has told the class that he is a Jewish convert, and it has piqued Stephanie's interest.

"You mean, 'Morgenbesser'? No, it's my name."

"But Morgenbesser's a Jewish name, isn't it?"

"German."

"It sounds Jewish to me," Stephanie insists, as if Morgenbesser may be lying to her or just doesn't know the origin of his own name. It's hard for Stephanie to acknowledge another authority; she spends her day supervising her five young children like the trail boss in a western roundup. Despite her name, Stephanie is not Jewish. Morgenbesser had felt a pang of disappointment when he learned that the "Stephanie Roth" on his class roster was not a Jewish girl. She's Catholic. Roth—a name that swings both ways.

Actually, Stephanie has a more complicated background. Her mother was Jewish; her father was Catholic. Her father ran out on the family when she was a child, and they took their mother's name, Rosen, as their family name, but they adopted their father's religion. It was probably Christmas that tilted the choice. Stephanie writes glowing essays about her anticipation of the season, the purchase of a tree, the hanging of stockings, and even makes comments about our savior, Jesus Christ.

"Honest, it's German. But there are a lot of German-sounding Jewish names, you know. Weisbaum, Feldman." He gestures vaguely to include "Roth." "Yiddish is a German dialect."

* * *

"Morgenbesser. That's a German name, isn't it?"

Kiddush in the social hall at the synagogue after Saturday morning services. Noah Rosenbloom has just become a bar mitzvah. Morgenbesser finds himself at a table with Jacob Matz and his Israeli-born wife, Chana. Is it his imagination, or is Matz' question more than simple curiosity about the origin of his name? Does he have a more sinister intent?

"It means 'a better tomorrow,'" he replies, smiling all around the table at the others. Eight people sit around the circular table, including the Matzes and Morgenbesser's wife, Amy.

"But it is German, isn't it?"

"Or maybe Dutch."

"Your family is from Bavaria?"

"Near Holland, actually, but it's been about a hundred and fifty years since my great-grandfather emigrated. Joined the California Gold Rush." Morgenbesser hates himself for the unspoken subtext of his statement, denying his family were Nazis, had long since become Americans.

"Did he?" Matz turns his attention away, no longer interested.

"But I still have relatives over there," Morgenbesser adds as a subtle "fuck you."

* * *

"I'm a convert," Marybeth Naden confesses to Morgenbesser at Noah Rosenbloom's bar mitzvah. "Jeff's Jewish. We'd been married two years before I converted. I converted five years ago just before Rachel was born." She speaks to him as if she is speaking to an authentic Jew, a man born and raised in the faith, the tradition. Her confession carries with it her lack of familiarity with Jewish customs, the fact that after "shalom," she doesn't know many Hebrew words, can't speak the language or understand the prayers, her confusion about the laws of kashruth, incomprehensible rules about eating food.

"Did you convert because of that?"

"Partly. That's why I did when I did. If I were Jewish, Rachel would be Jewish since I'm the mother, and it's a matrilineal thing, and we'd already decided that if we had any children they'd be raised Jewish."

"Did a rabbi marry you?"

"We had a hard time finding one who would. Finally this Reform rabbi, Steven Feit, agreed to marry us when we told him our children would be raised Jewish. Jeff didn't actually want any kids, but he's glad we have Rachel."

"I'm a convert, too," Morgenbesser says. He aims to be reassuring, but he is not sure if the expression in Marybeth's eyes when he says this is more like disappointment. Did she just squander her confession on the wrong person? She excuses herself and leaves the table. Morgenbesser wishes he'd kept his mouth shut.

* * *

"At work I try not to let the other Jews know I'm a convert," Morgenbesser tells Ellen Herxheimer on the exercise bikes. "I feel like it might let them down somehow. My dirty little secret."

"Let them down? How?"

"As if it diminishes my authenticity, my pedigree."

"Do you *feel* Jewish?"

"Well, I'm a little unsure what it means to 'feel' Jewish. To 'feel' anything, particularly, besides hot or cold or hungry."

"I *feel* Jewish," Ellen says, "but I also feel a bit of 'diminished authenticity' on account of my atheism and my non-participation in Jewish life; don't belong to a synagogue, for instance, not since my daughter had her bat mitzvah ten years ago. But at heart, yeah, I guess I do *feel* Jewish. It's a factor in my discouraging my daughter from marrying this very sweet non-Jewish man she met in college, in fact."

"The non-Jews at work are ambivalent about my status, too, the ones who know I'm a convert. There's this one guy, a redneck, who told me, 'Dan, I'm as Jewish as you are.' When I told him I'd converted, he said he was planning on converting to African-American. Only he used a different word."

"The ones who don't know?"

"Regard me as this strange exotic being who doesn't celebrate Christmas. It's Christmas that's the big defining factor, after all. Not just because it celebrates the birth of Christ, but because of the whole consumer season that's grown around it."

"How did your parents react?"

"They didn't have any problem with it."

"What about Christmas?"

"We still exchange gifts."

***

In the grocery store on the way home from the gym, Morgenbesser steps into the checkout lane where Joanne is scanning the packages and ringing up the purchases. Joanne is enormous. He's seen her here over the years as she has grown and grown. Originally a chubby young woman in her early twenties, she has ballooned to the point where her skin seems stretched and ready to pop; she's aged, too, and now in her late-thirties no longer has the redeeming sexual allure of her youth. The store management has decked their cashiers out in holiday duds, red caps with white tassels, and Joanne sure looks the part of a portly Santa doling out the gifts.

When it comes his turn to pay for his groceries, Morgenbesser smiles and nods at Joanne who, though she certainly recognizes him—once he'd returned a packaged pizza pie because it was green with mold when he removed it from its plastic sheath, and Joanne had let him exchange it for a new one, no questions asked, even though he did not have a sales receipt—treats him with the same impersonality that she treats all the customers.

"Getting cold out," he comments.

"Mmm," she agrees without looking up, dragging his packages over the glass barcode reader. "Got your Christmas shopping almost done?" Joanne asks him.

The Tenth Man

Morgenbesser walks through the metal detector at work. It reminds him of the chuppah under which he and Amy were married. Only, the marriage canopy did not object to his keys and coins. He steps back through, the alarm ringing again, and empties his pockets. Then he walks back through again. Silence. The black security guard nods him on to the turnstile where he waves his security badge at an electric eye and punches in his private code. The latch clicks and he is able to push his way through into the lobby. At last he can go to the elevators and ultimately to his desk.

What strikes Morgenbesser as absurd about the metal detector is that the federal employees do not have to pass through it, only the contractors. Something to do with the union, he understands. But you could hardly call it a fail safe security system, could you?

Especially when you consider some of the federal workers, he thinks, looking at Steve Gordon breezing past the security guards to the federal employee turnstiles. Steve is a scruffy young guy with a set of eyebrow rings that makes Morgenbesser think of a shower curtain rod, and spiked hair dyed a blinding shade of blond. Tattoos trail up and down his arms like animal tracks, peace symbols and flowers; he even has a tat on his cheek of a small butterfly. Like a sixties hippie born too late. But for all that, Gordon's probably not a danger to anybody, though he is supposed to be some sort of computer wizard from M.I.T. and could conceivably bring the agency to its knees if he wanted to.

Morgenbesser rides the elevator to the fifth floor where he walks down a maze of corridors to the cubicle where Mary, the company secretary, presides over the logbook he must sign when he arrives at work and when he leaves each day.

"Raining out yet?" Mary asks. She's a fat woman with beehive hair dyed a flaming orange.

"Not yet, but it's getting cloudier," Morgenbesser tells her. There are no windows in the building, so nobody knows what the weather is like outside.

"Supposed to rain today. Chance of thunderstorms."

"Yeah, that's what I heard," Morgenbesser agrees, and then he goes back to the elevators to descend to the fourth floor, where his own desk is, in one of several hundred cubicles set up like a refugee camp.

* * *

"Dan, we need you for the minyan." Josh Polansky, a heavyset guy with a thick mustache, looms over Morgenbesser, who sits at his computer typing away at a report. It's just after lunch. About half a dozen Orthodox Jewish guys have started organizing a mid-day minyan to recite the minchah prayers. Or maybe they've been doing it all along and Morgenbesser has just been made aware of it via Bernie Potts' e-mail broadcast.

Bernie himself is not Orthodox. A short, squat, gnomish man in his mid-fifties, Bernie has confided to Morgenbesser that he'd prefer to play bridge with his cronies in the fifth floor lounge when the minyan is taking place, but he's glad to fill in when they need a tenth man. Bernie set up the e-mail list at the request of Seth Friedman, one of the Orthodox dudes who wear kippot at all times. Yarmulkes, skullcaps.

Since the Orthodox dudes run the minyan, it's only Jewish males who are allowed to attend, and they have a tough time fielding the required ten male Jewish bodies. Morgenbesser has been the tenth man on occasion, the final body that enables the others to do their praying.

One Thursday they could only come up with nine, and

they'd disbanded without reading the prayers, though Morgenbesser suspects the real reason they did not persevere until they got a tenth was that Seth Friedman had not come. Everybody called Seth Sammy because his Hebrew name was Shmuel. Sammy was the one who brought the bag full of kippot and siddurim, the prayerbooks, and without the prayerbooks, how could you pray? Morgenbesser packs his own kippah these days, keeps one handy in the drawer of his desk, one he scarfed from a kid's bar mitzvah last winter, freebees offered to guests to commemorate the event. Have yarmulke, will travel. Like a knight errant from chivalric literature. Paladin.

Once they've got all ten guys, Ted Kaplan usually leads them in prayers. Facing the eastern wall of the conference room they've reserved, he davans like a dervish, bobbing and swaying in place while he mutters the Hebrew prayers at an amazing rate, lifting up on his tiptoes with the kadosh, kadosh, kadosh, bowing and ducking like a courtier. It's the best Morgenbesser can do to recognize an occasional prayer (*yit-gadaal, v'yit-kadash, sh'may rabah*...the kaddish prayer goes licking past his ears like a movie in fast motion) and to utter the odd "amen" at the appropriate interval.

"Just a second." Morgenbesser saves the text he has been working on, logs off of the computer and rises from his desk. He follows Josh as he weaves down the corridors of cubicles to the fourth floor conference room.

"Thanks a lot, Dan," Josh says over his shoulder. "We only have eight so far." The minyan was scheduled to begin five minutes ago. "We're running a little late," he continues, "but we're on Jewish time, so it don't matter." He chuckles. Josh is about as skilled at praying and recognizing Hebrew as Morgenbesser. His son became a bar mitzvah the year before, though, so he's been through the synagogue wringer recently, steeped in the protocol. Like Morgenbesser, he basically sees himself as an enabler; his presence as the tenth man allows the fervent davaners to proceed, and he basks in their performance by reflection. It's a mitzvah, a good deed.

They pass Myra Goldstein on their way to the conference room. A tough-talking sixty-ish woman with dyed red hair, Myra runs a little group of technicians who go around fixing people's computers. They call her Mama, like the leader of a little band of hoodlums, which is how Morgenbesser thinks of her. A ringleader, a "boss." As they nod at each other, he reflects that Myra's more Jewish than he is, only a convert; even if you can't "really" measure such things, and no Jew is "really" more Jewish than another, still, she comes from a long line of Jews. How convenient it would be for the dudes if they only let women join. But to Sammy and Ted and the others, that would be like saying you could have a minyan with five or eight—just as much an anathema. Ten men—ten *Jewish* men—was just the way it was. They didn't write the rulebook, after all. God did that. Hashem.

Morgenbesser kind of likes the men's club atmosphere. It's a cross between a locker room and a library. All the men are studious, serious, subdued—but there is an unmistakable male camaraderie. While they wait for the minchah prayers to get underway, their talk is unremarkable but spoken without the slightest hint of flirtation or sexual competitiveness, as there might be in a mixed crowd. No gallant guys. They speak indifferently, with the matter-of-fact modesty of men talking to men.

Sammy and several of the dudes are sitting at the conference table when Josh and Morgenbesser enter the room. Nine men, counting the new arrivals.

"Anybody seen Bernie?" Elliott Rosenthal asks.

"He's in Chicago for the next couple of weeks," Sammy says. "What about Shlomo?"

"Shlomo's out today," Mark Stainman says. "There's a message on his voice mail." Shlomo Cohen can usually be depended on. He's one of the dudes.

"What about Marty?"

"Give him a call."

Sammy calls Marty Levitsky on his cell phone but doesn't get an answer.

"I'm gonna go see if I can't find somebody," Josh says. He leaves the room, reducing the number to eight. A man on a mission.

"The security team has a meeting here at 1:30," Ron Plotkin announces. Plotkin glances at his wristwatch. It's five to one. The hourglass is running out. The prayers take about ten, fifteen minutes to perform.

"You still with security?" Stainman asks him.

"CICS, but they're always calling me and sending e-mail messages."

"When'd you join CICS?"

"A year ago. Last fall."

"Huh, I didn't know that."

"Who's Josh looking for? Anybody in particular?"

"Who is there?"

"Roman or Gennady, maybe?" The Russians, men who escaped the Soviet Union where Jew was essentially something stamped on an identity card. To Morgenbesser, they seem uncomfortable among the dudes, self-conscious and unsure how to behave around such fervent praying.

"You hear the one about the Jew who went to China?" Marvin Miller asks. It sounds like a joke, but then, Marvin, a kind of clownish-looking near-sighted bald guy, always sounds as if he's about to deliver a punchline. He fills up the expectant silence. "He's walking around the streets of Hong Kong when he hears the sound of Jews praying. He can't believe his ears. They're chanting the kaddish prayer. He goes down this little flight of stairs, the sound growing louder, and into this basement room, and sure enough, there are about a dozen men praying. He's overcome with emotion and asks if he can join. So one of the Chinese gentlemen comes up to him and says,

'You Jewish?'" Marvin lampoons a Chinese accent. "He says yes, and the Chinaman says, 'Funny, you don't *look* Jewish.'"

Polite laughter ripples around the room. It's a joke they've heard before. Morgenbesser wonders if this is somehow directed at him.

"One o'clock," Plotkin announces. Tick, tick, tick.

Just then the door pushes open, and Josh Polansky enters, with Steve Gordon in tow. *Steve Gordon!* Eyebrow rings, tattoos and all!

"Okay, we've got ten!" Josh announces triumphantly.

Everybody seems about as surprised as Morgenbesser by the tenth man. He hadn't known Gordon was Jewish, and apparently neither did the others. Ted is facing the eastern wall looking around as if for direction. Ron Plotkin glances again at his wristwatch. Mark Stainman looks around to see how the others are reacting.

Morgenbesser is the first to take a prayerbook from the bag.

God is Everything, Mostly

"This is like something out of *The Rocky Horror Picture Show*," Amy Morgenbesser observes, bemused. She is a tallish woman with rusty red hair, striking to look at from a distance, but up close her face takes on something of a doll's blank look. Her husband has spent the past twenty years trying to decide if she is pretty or not. The woman for whom he converted to Judaism, in order to marry her. His wife, the literature professor.

"Arriving at the haunted castle on a dark and stormy night?"

"Exactly. The Christmas lights don't help, either."

The Morgenbessers have driven more than an hour through a December rainstorm to The Mount, a conference center in rural Maryland, to spend the Jewish Sabbath at a b'nai mitzvah retreat. Their daughter Natalie is going to become a bat mitzvah in a year; her younger sister Eve is with them as well. After work, they picked the kids up from school, packed a bag and joined the rush hour traffic. The conference center, an enormous light display on the brick wall at the edge of the campus declaring, MERRY CHRISTMAS in blinking red, white and green, is a former Catholic girls' college that has been taken over by an outfit called the Church of the Brothers of the Crucified Christ, an obscure ascetic sect with remote ties to the Mennonites, or so Morgenbesser understands. It offers itself as a retreat for churches and other religious and non-profit groups. On a marquee in front of the main building, a small sign welcomes the Beth Chaim Synagogue. About seventeen families are expected.

The Morgenbessers pull their Geo Prizm into a parking space and run across the asphalt, hunkered over in the rain like soldiers running across a battlefield. Rabbi Leon Weisbaum, a lanky figure in jeans and sneakers, greets them by the Christmas tree in the lobby next to the registration desk behind which the two conference center hosts sit in an official pose that reminds Morgenbesser of Grant Woods' *American Gothic*. Or is it just Amy's observation about the Frankenstein movie spoof that makes him nervous? And the stormy night outside.

"Sorry we're late," Morgenbesser begins; it's long past sundown, after all, but Rabbi Weisbaum cuts him short.

"Not at all! You're one of the first to arrive! Dinner won't be ready until six. Why don't you go to your rooms and relax? Let me introduce you to Mel and Janet, our hosts." Rabbi Weisbaum seems a little *too* enthusiastic to Morgenbesser, who has already pegged Mel and Janet as "Riff Raff" and "Magenta."

"Welcome to the Mount," Riff Raff says in a frail whispery voice that makes Morgenbesser think of spiders, while the rabbi's voice booms over him in an aggressively reassuring tone. *Methinks he doth protest too much!*

"Mel and Janet have your room keys and nametags all ready. You're already pre-registered so you don't have to sign any papers or anything."

Magenta has removed the envelopes marked "Morgenbesser" from a folder and hands them to Amy. They contain room keys and meal tickets and helpful information about the campus grounds.

"Of course, Natalie will be staying over in the other building—"

"Trinity," Riff Raff whispers.

"Yes, Trinity," Rabbi Weisbaum says, unable to completely squash the irony from his generally good-humored tone. "Daniel and Amy and Evie, your room is right here in this building."

"Two-o-five," Morgenbesser says, reading the number on the key his wife gives him.

"Why don't we all go over to the other building—"

"Trinity," Morgenbesser says with a smile.

"Yes, and we'll take a look at Natalie's room. She's sharing a room with Katie Ratner, I believe."

"Hope you enjoy your stay at the Mount," Riff Raff whispers, and they head out the door into the pelting rainstorm to take Natalie to her room.

* * *

The purpose of the b'nai mitzvah retreat is to acquaint all of the families with one another. These are the boys and girls who will become bar and bat mitzvah during the next calendar year. They all go to different schools in the city and they are even in different grades, some in sixth and some in seventh. Natalie Morgenbesser is only in the fifth grade. The rabbi would like the children to develop lasting friendships among themselves and even the families to become more familiar with one another. Kind of like being in summer camp and having to pair off with strangers (Morgenbesser's initial reaction).

"Not bad," Morgenbesser says when he and Amy and Evie enter their room. Two queen-sized beds on one side of the spacious room, two singles on the other. Two bathrooms, two showers.

"A lot better than Natalie's."

"Hers looked comfortable enough, though. The idea is to make friends with the other kid. What's her name? Kathy?"

"Katie. There aren't any Kathys any more. They're all Katies."

Morgenbesser pulls aside the bedspread to lie down. In the middle of the white sheet, a dead brown field mouse is curled up like a turd.

"Oh Jesus. Look at that."

Amy gasps, puts her hand to her mouth. Evie screams.

*　*　*

"Well, they changed the sheets. That guy apologized all over the place. I felt kind of sorry for him."

"Mel."

Riff Raff. "Yeah, I couldn't remember his name. He had no idea how the mouse got there." Morgenbesser sounds dubious.

"It's unfortunate," the rabbi sympathizes. They're lounging around the dining room with six other families, waiting for the others to arrive. "But everything's okay now?"

Morgenbesser shrugs.

"They seem really helpful. They're a retired couple. They live here year-round, welcoming guests." Weisbaum seems to feel genuinely responsible for the mouse, and Morgenbesser in turn feels responsible for the rabbi's discomfort.

"They changed the sheets and got rid of the mouse, so I guess it's all right. Amy was a little freaked, and Evie got scared."

"And *you* looked like you were going to be sick," Amy says.

"Yeah, Daddy," Evie chimes in, annoyed by the way her father characterizes her reaction to the mouse.

"Well, I'm glad it's resolved," Weisbaum says, forcing closure on the situation and turning his attention to the room.

"I guess we'd better start now. They want us out of the dining room by 7:30. The others can join us when they arrive. Did everybody bring shabbos candles?"

They sit two families apiece at the long cafeteria tables, each family wrapped up in its own cloud, casting furtive glances at the others. After a while, unable to bear the self-consciousness, Morgenbesser sticks his hand out at the father of the family with whom they are sitting. The man seems likewise relieved and warmly shakes Morgenbesser's hand.

"Roman Belotserkovsky," he says in a thick accent, needlessly adding, "We're Russian. This is my wife, Faina and my son, Michael."

Morgenbesser basks in Roman's evident relief. He introduces Amy, Natalie and Eve. But then the rabbi announces it is time to go up to the conference rooms.

* * *

The dozen families who've actually come meet in one of the conference rooms upstairs that's been reserved for the Beth Chaim guests. Several activities have been planned for the evening to help everybody become better acquainted. There's a brief discussion of the next day's parshe, which is about Joseph interpreting Pharaoh's dream of the seven fat cows and the seven lean cows, the seven fat ears of corn and seven scrawny ears. Then there's a "stroll through the scroll" session during which the rabbi unfurls the Torah scroll and everybody gets a firsthand look at it. Up close and personal. Then there's a session of singing songs.

Midway through the evening activities, several of the Brothers of the Crucified Christ knock gently at the door, looks of mild concern on their faces. Riff Raff and Magenta are with them. The rabbi goes out to consult with them while inside the adults fuss over their children to avoid feeling awkward among the others. Some make polite observations about the beauty and majesty of the Torah scroll.

When Weisbaum returns, he tells everybody that he has just learned that the Brothers of the Crucified Christ forbid the consumption of alcoholic beverages at the Mount conference center. They were evidently shocked to find several empty wine bottles that the congregation had used for the Friday night kiddush.

"I didn't realize this," Rabbi Weisbaum apologizes. "It must have been in the contract but I didn't read it. We'll just have to use a substitute for any prayers involving wine. We ought to respect our hosts' religious practices."

"Talk about respecting others' religious practices," Richard

Karpay mutters. "You'd think maybe they'd—" But he doesn't finish his sentence. Doesn't have to.

"They're really quite gracious about it," Weisbaum says. "They aren't being nasty. But we ought to respect their rules."

A few minutes later, while the rabbi is pointing out some of the places where the Torah scroll has been repaired and the implications this has on the calligraphy, they hear a bloodcurdling scream out in the hallway, and everybody rushes to the door, alarmed.

Magenta is standing out in the hallway amid a pool of coffee. She has been setting up the evening snack buffet and accidentally dropped the urn, spilling coffee all over, scalding her leg. Riff Raff is busy mopping up.

If the purpose of the retreat is to bring the families together, it seems to be working. They are starting to feel trapped and circled.

* * *

When they crawl into bed, exhausted, Morgenbesser is unable to fall asleep. Amy slumbers beside him, and across the room, Evie is curled up in a fetal ball, sound asleep, but Morgenbesser imagines he hears mice in the woodwork, imagines he feels them scurrying under the covers, their whiskers tickling his bare legs.

Eventually, he does fall asleep, but it's a fitful sleep, full of wild, vivid dreams. In one, Riff Raff and Magenta are leading a horde of faceless Brothers of the Crucified Christ on a rampage through the dormitory, a modern-day pogrom here at the Mount. Amy is yanked from their room, naked, a towel wrapped around her breasts and hips. *Yes! She really is beautiful!* He lunges after her, to save her, and then the scene shifts and they are in the cafeteria, lined up as before a firing squad, Riff Raff strutting in front of them Nazi-style. Magenta is dragging something into the room. He can't tell what it is, but it is slowly dawning on him that these are some sort of torture devices and they'd all better get the hell out of there quickly, when he feels something brush his leg and, awakening with a start, sure it's a mouse, he finds Evie crawling into bed with them. She too, has been having trouble sleeping.

* * *

The next day begins with breakfast in the dining room and then they're off to the conference room for the Shabbat service. Natalie looks a little grim when she comes in. Her roommate, Katie Ratner, evidently left their room to join two of her classmates from middle school in an adjoining room, and Natalie spent the night alone, lonely. When Natalie reaches the end of the cafeteria line with her tray of pancakes, cereal and orange juice, Magenta asks for her meal ticket. She does not have one. She left her meal tickets back in her room.

"You can't have breakfast without a meal ticket," Magenta says pleasantly, but as this entails going all the way back to Trinity, her parents, Dan and Amy, quite reasonably suggest they will bring it later. Even the rabbi pops in and assures the Morgenbessers this will be all right. But Magenta's eyes, meanwhile, seem to have become hands tightening around the rabbi's windpipe.

* * *

Up in the conference room, the rabbi has another activity for the group before the Shabbat service begins. It's all in the spirit of approaching the Torah together. He explains that a midrash is a commentary on Torah text that sheds light on unanswered questions, and he asks everybody to create a midrash on the parshe to clarify the meaning of the story of Joseph unraveling the Pharaoh's dream. The rules are that they can use only four different colors—including the background color of the paper—and they must show five things in the picture—God, Pharaoh, Joseph, the dream, and themselves. Then, they must explain their pictures to the rest of the group. It's an exercise Weisbaum has cribbed from a religious retreat handbook.

Morgenbesser is reminded of a talkshow he recently saw at the health club while he was riding the exercise bicycle. A handsome blonde woman with a microphone was grilling several couples who sat in folding chairs on the stage, the studio audience firing questions at them. The theme of the show was that perennial favorite, bedroom problems. An enormous fat woman with six or eight chins and a permanent scowl complained that her husband refused to have sex with her. The husband, meanwhile, a skinny little guy with a raggedy mustache, denied that he refused to have sex. "There just isn't ever an opportunity," he insisted. The lady with the mike (she called herself "Doctor" Somebody. Joan? Liz? Pam? A monosyllabic name) wasn't letting him off the hook that easily, though. She questioned him about impotence, fidelity, a lack of compassion. In the end, the man had to hug the fat woman and kiss her before the studio audience, who howled their approval. Of course, they were certainly being paid for the performance, but still, it made Morgenbesser feel uncomfortable, seeing these people put on the spot. Entertainment marketed as therapy.

Similarly, Weisbaum puts the kids on the spot when they describe their drawings. Why did you make Pharaoh blue? Why are the seven fat cows in the center of the picture? Where are you in relation to the scene? Etc. The boys tend to act like clowns, their responses on the faultline between wit and insolence. The girls more often than not seem mortified. When Natalie compares the story to Goldilocks and the Three Bears—the meal of one too hot and that of the other too cold but the last one just right—the rabbi seems a little uncomfortable with the comparison of the bible story to a fairytale—but he lets it slide. Still, Natalie senses his displeasure and tries to backtrack. But this only makes it worse.

"I guess you can't really say that. I mean, the three bears and the seven cows. That doesn't even add up! It's just not..."

"No, no!" Weisbaum insists good-naturedly. "This is very insightful. Both seven and three are important numbers. Three patriarchs, what else? Four. Four is an important number. Think of the Haggadah. Four sons, four questions, four cups of wine. Gamatria generally is a significant part of Judaism, the numerical value of Hebrew letters. And the fairytale itself is a sort of dream that can be interpreted." But it's just adding a layer of words to the situation and fails to alleviate the child's self-consciousness. Weisbaum switches gears.

"And where is God in the picture?" he asks, trying to smooth it over.

"God's the whole picture," Natalie says, and suddenly she is unsure if this might also be a stupid thing to say or even blasphemous. "God's everything, mostly," she finally blurts, trying to explain her meaning.

"Very good, Natalie," Weisbaum says, and seeing that the best solution is to turn the spotlight away from her, he lets her off the hook. "Well, I guess we'd better move on to the service, which we'll have to shorten since the cafeteria's only going to be open for lunch from 12:00 to 1:00." He glances significantly at his watch.

The service is indeed a short one, just a few warmup prayers, one mass aliyah of the b'nai mitzvah class during the Torah service, which the rabbi reads at lightning speed, and barely a moment's added reflection to the amidah. They wind up with the mourners' kaddish and a spirited rendition of "Adon Olam." Trouble is, they are a little *too* expeditious about completing the service, and there are still a few minutes before they can go down to the cafeteria. They've already been warned by Riff Raff and Magenta that they should *not* expect to come early; they'll just get in the way of the hosts' chores.

So to pass the time, Karen Burstein, the Sunday school

teacher, leads them in song. She makes all the b'nai mitzvah children come up and sing. Thinking she is honoring Natalie, who has just been put through the wringer, Karen asks her to lead the congregation in singing "Rise and Shine." Natalie groans and rolls her eyes; she is familiar with the song for its having been lampooned so emphatically on *The Simpsons*. Of all the forced activities, this one tops them all for her! This is the proverbial straw that breaks the camel's back. She looks like she would like to flee. Karen starts the clapping.

The Lord said to Noah,
There's gonna be a floody, floody

Seeing his daughter's distress, Morgenbesser winks at her to get her to smile, a sign of their complicity. But Sandy Rosenthal, mother of Noah, thinks Morgenbesser is winking at *her*, and she winks back, but then Joel Richman mistakes this for a wink at *him*, and *he* winks in turn. Roman Belotserkovsky intercepts the wink and warmly passes it on, back to Morgenbesser, who winks at Amy. *Yes, she really is pretty!* Morgenbesser decides, winking at her. Soon, the whole room is full of people winking at one another, and Natalie can barely restrain her laughter.

The sun came out
And dried up the landy landy.
Rise and shine
And give God your glory, glory...

Guard My Tongue

Christmas falls on a Saturday this year, and Amy's younger sister, Jackie, has come down from New York with her son, Jacob, to spend the weekend. Christmas is a hard day for anybody to get through, but for Jews it can be especially tough, because it's so boring. Nothing is open; nothing to do. Jackie is particularly vocal about how tedious the day is, and it feels to Morgenbesser as though she aims her remarks at him, holds *him* responsible. Under the onslaught of Jackie's derision, Morgenbesser feels like a traitor about to be exposed for harboring disloyal emotions. His memories of Christmas are not so bad, after all. He'd been with his family; they'd exchanged gifts, had had a festive meal. He can't quite muster the outsider's feelings of resentment and ridicule.

Jackie never has quite bought Morgenbesser's "conversion"; how can you "become" a Jew? It's an ethnicity, almost racial, and she regards him as hopelessly goyish, particularly since he grew up in the Midwest. Morgenbesser can feel her eyes following him around the kitchen all morning while Amy helps Natalie and Evie get ready for services.

"You're going with them?" she asks.

"Well yeah, sure," he says, his voice rising ever so slightly in a kind of tight defensive whine. "I usually do. Almost always."

"Really? And you're able to follow it?" Jackie's cool put-down. Of course, Morgenbesser understands the service as much as anybody whose native language is English.

"More or less. How about you?" he asks, shifting the spotlight. "You coming?"

Jackie gives him a look that makes him blush. *Are you*

serious? She says, "I'd better stay here in case Paul calls." Jacob, however, wants to go with his cousins, so Jackie will stay home by herself. Her husband, Paul Porter, rarely accompanies his wife on her infrequent trips to Baltimore. Not that he dislikes the Morgenbessers, but he has problems with allergies, and the Morgenbessers' cats—or cat, the older one, Sophie, having died in November—are particularly vexing to him. In no time at all, Paul is a wheezing, sneezing mess in their home, tears streaming down his face, eyes red, nose running. He does not complain but he's in evident agony. The Morgenbessers do not hold it against him that he does not want to come.

"I'll tell you what the *parshe* was all about when we get back," Morgenbesser says, and Jackie gives a sardonic little chuckle. According to Amy, Jackie loathes religious services, refuses to attend, though now that her son is seven years old, she's started to mellow somewhat. She's determined that he become a bar mitzvah. But for years she was notorious for missing services and for her general non-observance.

* * *

There's a guest speaker at Beth Chaim from Chana today, the organization that looks out for battered Jewish women. Only a few dozen people are present, and services are held in the small chapel. Not even the rabbi is here; he's gone with his family to Florida. Services are run by Herb Garber, a member of the congregation. After the Torah service, in place of a sermon, Herb introduces the guest speaker.

Sally Rosen is a slight, tense-looking woman. Her small dark eyes dart around the room like a trapped animal's. Morgenbesser wonders if she's been a victim of abuse herself, if that's how she has become involved with the organization. She's dressed in a pinstriped business outfit, and she holds a sheaf of papers that looks to Morgenbesser like a prepared speech.

"Good shabbos," she begins, looking around the room, and then, sure enough, she launches into the prepared speech: "Why does wife abuse occur?" she asks rhetorically. "There are many theories to explain this. The Feminist Theory explains spouse abuse in terms of the social structure, the subordination of women. The patriarchal nature of society is reinforced with spousal abuse; it's a way of keeping women in their place. There's also the so-called Culture of Violence Theory, which states that in a society where violence is accepted as a means to solve conflicts, spouse abuse gets tacit approval. The Sex-Role Theory is similar to the Feminist Theory; little girls are socialized to become the victims of little boys, a self-perpetuating cycle that continues into adulthood. The Intergenerational Transmission Theory states that individuals who observe or experience violence in the home are likely to use it themselves. Men who observe their fathers abusing their mothers are likely to abuse their wives..."

Morgenbesser looks at several of the other men in the congregation. They are fidgeting in their seats, squirming. Is this guilt? An urge to argue? His mind starts to wander, stray from Sally's speech. He thinks back on dinner the night before.

* * *

"Do Natalie and Evie think of themselves as Jewish?" Jackie asks Amy as they sit down to eat.

"Does Jacob?" Morgenbesser asks, but Jackie ignores his sarcastic tone.

"Well, of course they do," Amy replies, confused by her sister's question. "They go to a Jewish day school. Natalie's about to become a bat mitzvah."

"What about Dan's family?"

"What about them?"

"Don't Natalie and Evie identify with them?"

"They know their religion."

Jackie does not pursue the conversation, and Morgenbesser assumes she's made her point.

"There's a group of very Orthodox guys at work whose minyan I join after lunch most days," Morgenbesser says, reaching for the salt. While not very religious herself, Jackie becomes defensive about Jews and Judaism around Morgenbesser, as if he is an interloper, a carpetbagger. Sensing this, he likes to drop irreverent remarks to rile her up. "You know, the guys who walk around with the Boy George hats."

"They let you join them?"

"Well, yeah, I guess I enable them."

"No! *They* enable *you*," Jackie says. The shrill tone is like a pack of dogs straining at the leash, under control but dying to break loose.

"No, no, *I* enable *them*," Morgenbesser corrects. "They can't do their thing without ten men, so my presence allows them to perform."

"They don't question your Jewishness?"

"They don't ask for a pedigree, if that's what you mean."

"They don't check to make sure you're circumcised?"

"How would you tell a Jewish circumcision from a non-Jewish one?" Amy asks. She does not seem to notice her sister's aggression, which seems all too nakedly apparent to Morgenbesser. To Amy, Jackie is the irreverent kid sister who has always found religion cloying and claustrophobic. Amy believes Jackie is skeptical of Morgenbesser's conversion because she can't understand why anybody would want to observe such practices, let alone choose to do so.

* * *

"Why do women remain in abusive relationships?" Sally asks, segueing to her next topic. "Psychologists have noted a three-stage pattern of abuse. First, there's a tension-building stage. It's sort of an enabling stage. The husband gets cranky and indignant, makes slighting remarks, finds fault with his wife. He grumbles, complains, insults, disparages, finds fault. Wife abusers typically have low self-esteem and negative self-concepts. But the wife will often let her husband know that she accepts the blame for his rage; perhaps she feels sorry for him because she knows he regards himself as a loser. She tells *herself* that the battering she's received before could have been much worse.

"This stage gives way to the one involving an acute battering incident. The husband erupts violently, hits her, throws something at her. It's more than just threats; it's active, brutal, physical violence, resulting in a broken arm or a broken jaw.

"When the results of the violence occur, that's when the third stage happens. The 'honeymoon' stage, as it's called." Sally's voice breaks with the irony. She wipes her eyes. "It's a period of kindness, contrition, loving behavior. He breaks her collarbone and then apologizes. 'Honey, I'll never, *ever* do that to you again,' he promises, and she believes him. Even after the tenth or twentieth time she goes on believing him, *wanting* to believe him. Victimization not only entails immediate suffering, you see, but an acquired sense of helplessness and hopelessness—emotional numbness."

* * *

After dinner, as they clear the dishes for dessert, Jackie turns to Morgenbesser and asks, "Have you ever had apple pie with a slice of cheese on it?"

It strikes Morgenbesser as an odd question, and it takes him a moment before he begins to mutter an inconclusive answer. "Oh, maybe. I don't know. Probably. I'm not sure."

"My friend Carol from Wisconsin says it's a real goyish dessert."

"I don't know. It could be," Morgenbesser replies, taking an armload of dishes to the kitchen. He wonders why she does this, why she seems so intent on reminding him that he was not born Jewish. Maybe it's really part of her competitive relationship with Amy, diminishing her older sister's legitimacy by "exposing" her husband, a kind of Jacob-and-Esau dynamic, stealing the birthright of the first-born. Jackie's husband Paul's family are all old-time Orthodox Brooklyn Jews, dealers in diamonds and the stock market, though Paul, a journalist, is not very observant himself. Some of Paul's relatives perished in the Holocaust death camps; others had their property confiscated by the Nazis. But he does not seem to hold Morgenbesser's German ancestry against him—not his generation's concern. But could this help explain Jackie's attitude? Or is she simply a bitch?

* * *

"More than fifty percent of all women experience violence from intimate partners," Sally is saying, starting to rattle off the statistics now. "Wife-beating results in more injuries requiring medical attention than rape, auto accidents and muggings combined. Thirty percent of all women murdered in the United States are killed by their husbands, boyfriends, or ex-boyfriends." She lets the facts sink in before she continues. Turns the page.

"Christian women often feel compelled to stay in abusive relationships because of the scriptural mandate to 'submit to their husbands' and to 'turn the other cheek.' Jewish women, on the other hand, may feel pressure not to bring shame on their community in the eyes of the goyim by revealing the abuse; it's their responsibility to maintain *shalom bayit*, peace in the home. To bring attention to the abuse would be a *shande* in the eyes of the community, a shame. So they don't talk about it. They keep it hidden.

"Approximately twenty-five percent of all Jewish women are or have been in abusive relationships. Moreover, on average, Jewish women *stay* in abusive relationships twice as long as most women, simply because they *don't* talk about it."

Some of the men have been squirming and twitching restlessly in their seats all during Sally's talk, and when the question-and-answer period comes they explode like horses out of their gates.

"How many Jewish women have been killed in the Baltimore area during the past year?" Nathan Felser demands. He clearly feels affronted by Sally's remarks.

"How many women have been killed in the Baltimore area in the past year? Well, I don't know—"

"I mean, how many husbands have actually killed their wives—"

"I know of at least one whose husband shot her in a fit of rage."

"One? You say one?"

"Abuse is more than homicide. It's not always only physical abuse, either."

"One? One woman? And you call this a problem?"

"We receive calls every day from women whose husbands terrorize them, lock them up in their apartments—"

"But only one Jewish woman in the past *year* has actually been killed?"

"To my knowledge, but let me tell you, I know women whose husbands burn them with cigarettes, beat them with belts, hit them with chairs, women whose husbands don't even physically hurt them at all but hold them in such terror—"

Ira Levi has had his hand in the air for several minutes now, but he doesn't wait to be called on. "What about women abusing men? That happens a lot more often than you'd think, too! A friend of mine, his wife hit him so hard with a frying pan, he had to have stitches in his head. He practically got a concussion—"

There's only so much time for the post-Torah service discussion. If they ever want to have lunch and get on with the day, they have to cut it short. Herb Garber brings the discussion to an end, thanks Sally, and they proceed with the rest of the service, singing the prayers and praying silently during the Amidah.

As congregants conclude the Amidah, they sit in their seats. While he doesn't read the prayers or perform the special choreography of approaching and retiring, bowing and bobbing that goes with the Amidah, he likes to consider the translations. One of the prayers, "Guard My Tongue," in which the penitent asks God for restraint in speech, especially catches his attention. The translations vary from text to text. The prayerbooks the Orthodox dudes at work distribute read:

My God, guard my tongue from evil and my lips from speaking deceitfully.
To those who curse me, let my soul be silent,
And let my soul be like dust to everyone.

In the version the shul provides the translation reads:

Oh, Lord,
Guard my tongue from evil and my lips from speaking guile
And to those who slander me, let me give no heed.
May my soul be humble and forgiving to all.

Morgenbesser ponders over the differences, "speaking deceitfully" as opposed to "speaking guile." And if the nuances are insignificant, why not the alliterative, "guard my lips from speaking lies." Lips-lies. Would it make a difference? There are probably prayerbooks that do use the word "lies" instead of "deceit" or "guile." And the word "dust," he thinks, another curious word. "Let my soul be like dust" and "May my soul be humble." Humility and dust. Forgiveness and dust. Dust to dust. What could be more humble—more honest—than dirt? He thinks of Jackie's taunts and innuendo and wishes he could forgive her.

* * *

On the way home, Morgenbesser asks Amy what she thought of Nathan Felser's comments. Natalie and Evie and Jacob sit in the back, absorbed in some sort of game.

"Well, I guess the minute you open your mouth in a discussion like that you're going to put your foot in it, but was he really trying to say that because only one woman was murdered that spouse abuse isn't a problem?"

"Yeah, he really made an ass out of himself, didn't he? Did you notice all those guys there squirming self-consciously in their seats? I wasn't sure if it was guilt or anger. The only question I had was, how do they know Jewish women stay in abusive relationships twice as long as other women? How can you possibly measure that? I hate the way people twist statistics to make their point. Why bother with statistics at all when you're talking about abuse?"

When they arrive home, Natalie and Evie insist on showing Jacob a neighbor's house with an elaborate display of lights and Christmas decorations in the yard, so Amy takes them down the street while Morgenbesser enters the house through the basement door. Walking up the stairs to the dining room, the sound of Jackie's voice muffled behind the door arrests him. She seems to be pleading. He stops a moment before pushing the door open and listens, the urgent tone making him cautious.

"I'm sorry, Paul!" Jackie beseeches. "*Please* don't be angry with me! I didn't *mean* to wake you up! It's after twelve o'clock, after all. I'm *sorry*! I *promise* I'll never do it again!"

Morgenbesser leans back against the wall, wondering what to do.

"It's my fault, I *know*, Paul! But I didn't mean to do it, and I'll never do it again, I promise!"

Morgenbesser turns around and goes quietly back down into the basement and out the door. It's not forgiveness he feels, but when Amy and the kids come back, he makes sure they're all noisy going into the house.

Rosencrantz and Guildenstern Are Jews

Amy and Daniel Morgenbesser lie in bed, insomniacs. It is 3:00 a.m. Each senses the other is awake, but neither of them speaks, hoping to fall back asleep.

"Damn it," Morgenbesser mutters softly, remembering something.

"What?"

"You're awake?"

"Of course I'm awake. What's the matter?"

"I forgot the recyclables."

"You what?"

"The glass and cans and plastic recyclables. I forgot to take them out."

"I thought you said, 'sucking nipples.'"

Morgenbesser laughs. "Not a bad idea."

They lie quietly for a moment, pondering the implications, each stirred slightly by the possibility. But it seems like such an effort. What they really want is sleep.

"How was your class last night?" Amy finally asks.

"Not bad. We're reading *Hamlet*. Stephanie Roth wanted to know if Rosencrantz and Guildenstern were Jewish."

"What did you say?"

"It's an interesting question, but I wasn't sure it mattered one way or another."

"Hamlet's friends from his youth in Denmark. As Gertrude says, 'being of so young days brought up with him' and 'neighboured to his youth and haviour' or some such."

"Is there any evidence they were Jewish?"

"Only their names, I guess."

"Which could swing either way, like Stephanie's name, Roth, and she's not Jewish."

"They're not identified as Jewish in the play, and usually Christian writers made a point of pointing out when a character was Jewish; the fact was always significant. Take *The Merchant of Venice* or Marlowe's *The Jew of Malta*."

"Stories that feature Jews converting to Christianity."

"Abigail and Jessica."

"Even Shylock, at the end, is ordered by Antonio to 'presently become a Christian.'"

"Elizabethan England was preoccupied with the conversion of the Jews. Even obsessed. The conversion of the Jews was thought to be a necessary antecedent to Christ's Second Coming."

"According to the prevailing interpretation of the Book of Revelation or something, right? Well, there's plenty of Christian imagery in *Hamlet*."

"So you'd think, if Rosencrantz and Guildenstern *were* supposed to be Jewish, it would be explicitly stated somewhere by somebody."

"You'd think."

"Ever wonder what part of Antonio's body Shylock was going to get his pound of flesh from?"

"The breast, near his heart."

"In the late sixteenth century the word 'flesh' was often used as a euphemism for 'penis,' especially in the Bible. Shakespeare himself made puns on the word in *Romeo and Juliet*."

"But Shylock specifies the 'breast,' near his heart."

"Christian circumcision was 'of the heart' and not 'of the flesh.' Renaissance theologians emphasized that aspect of Paul's letter to the Romans. It's a kind of circumcision he's after. There was a lot of fear and fascination with Jewish circumcision in Elizabethan England, part of the obsession with the Jews. So it's simply another reference. Complicated, though."

"Yeah, I'm not sure I get it."

"Well, you take Shylock's literalism—"

"Forget it. I'm too tired. Let's try to get some sleep."

They lie quietly a moment, making an effort to achieve self-forgetfulness, unconsciousness. Then Morgenbesser breaks the silence.

"I like Stephanie. There are basically four kinds of students. There's the increasingly rare type that sees the teacher as the 'master' and the student as the disciple. Then there are those that see him as a cop to their criminal. Similarly, there are those who see the teacher as the 'boss' to their 'worker.' A guy more or less arbitrarily in charge. Then there are those who see themselves as customers and the teacher is this service provider, somebody they've 'hired' whose 'help' is always subject to scrutiny and evaluation. Stephanie is this type."

"And what does that have to do with Rosencrantz and Guildenstern being Jewish?"

"About as much as their Jewishness or non-Jewishness has to do with the play. They were simply sent for and got crushed in the collision of more powerful forces. As the Jews often were, come to think of it."

"I know that kind of student."

"The kind that gets crushed in the collision of powerful forces?"

"The customer mentality."

"The logical development in America, where we emphasize the earning-power of a college degree and the utility of factual knowledge. But what interests me about Stephanie is her religious orientation. Her mother was a Jew, and her father was a Catholic; the family took the father's religion, but when he ran out on the family, they took the mother's name, Rosen. But even then they kept the Catholic faith, even the mother. I wonder if Stephanie's interest in Rosencrantz and Guildenstern is for the similarity of names."

"Rosen and Rosencrantz."

"She puts down Jewish religion a lot, but I think she does it just to annoy me. The Passover food, the appeal of Chanukah versus Christmas, and so on."

"Or maybe the lady doth protest too much, to quote Gertrude?"

"You mean, she's insecure about her own religious identity and goes overboard to put down the Jews, to distance herself?"

"Something like that."

"Could be, I suppose."

They lie quietly a moment, and then Amy twists in bed to look at the ghostly display on the digital alarm clock, the lime-green neon letters glowing in the clock on the headboard.

"I am going to be so exhausted. And I've got to take Natalie to her bat mitzvah lesson tomorrow."

"Should we try to get some sleep?"

"I'd like to, but it may be hopeless."

But they fall silent again, until Morgenbesser remembers something.

"I got an e-mail today from Seth Friedman that the minyan is being discontinued until next October. Apparently with daylight savings time and the longer days the timing of the mid-day prayers has changed, or something. I'd kind of started looking forward to it. The men's club." He lies in bed vaguely wondering what it was about the minyan that appealed to him, what its intellectual appeal consisted of, and he remembers something else to tell Amy.

"Speaking of converted Jews and counterfeit Christians, Elliott Bortz was telling us at the last one about when he was a college student in Miami and used to bust up Jews-for-Jesus proselytizers who portrayed themselves as Jews but then, once they'd sung Havah Nagila and prayed with the unsuspecting elderly Jews who were their targets, they'd go into a hard sell for Jesus. A kind of deception. Bait and switch. Elliott said

A Better Tomorrow

they'd report these guys to hotel management, who were Jews, and get them kicked out."

"Jewish Christian converts pretending to be Jews to convert other Jews to Christianity. Sounds almost like Shakespearean cross-dressing, men playing women playing men."

"The English were suspicious of the authenticity of Jews becoming Christians. There's that scene in *The Merchant of Venice* where Antonio teases Jessica about it. This whole complicated identity thing about race and religion."

"It *is* very complicated when you look at it closely. What seems so clear and obvious on superficial inspection turns out to be a really tangled mess."

"When ultimately we're all just creatures that get born, live for a while and then die. I mean, if you don't take that redemption stuff seriously."

"Or put much stock in an afterlife."

"I've found that since I've become middle-aged, I read the obituaries with an eye to the age of the dead. On good days the dead people are all in their 80's or at least 70's. But disturbingly, many are 48 and 31 and 54. Today's announcements include James Shepherd, an on-air morning radio producer, dead at 35, colon cancer, Gerald Lutz, 59, a police officer, heart attack, Rita Gleason, 72, architect, ovarian cancer, Grace Carter, 73, former executive secretary, cancer, Michael Hopwood, 48, vice president for an investment firm, undermined causes. Those were just the ones written up. Then there's the potter's field page of obituaries, a full page of 8-point type of death notices that look like Personal Ads.

"And who's still alive? Well, Eudora Welty turned 91 today; Ben Nighthorse Campbell, the turncoat Republican senator from Colorado, hit 67. Tony Dow, who played Wally on *Leave It to Beaver*, turned 55. Chess Champ Gary Kasparov is 37. Rick Schroeder, the former child star who was the high-profile wet dream of some pederast or other a while back, if I recall correctly, turned 30 today. Thirty! It used to sound so old. Well, enough of this bitching and moaning about the inevitable. As they say, consider the alternative."

"Whatever that is."

"'…the dread of something after death, the undiscovered country, from which no traveler returns, puzzles the will, and makes us rather bear those ills we have…'"

"Act three, scene one, Hamlet's soliloquy." Amy lets out a big yawn. "I think I can maybe fall asleep now. To sleep, perchance to dream. Let's try."

Morgenbesser rolls over. But before he closes his eyes he says, "Try to remind me about the recylcables in the morning, will you?"

A Hint of Figs

"What utter bullshit!" Morgenbesser's tone mingles contempt and frustration. In any case, it exceeds the provocation. Amy looks up, startled. She has been tidying up the dining room in preparation for Shabbat. Natalie and Evie are outside playing with the neighbors. Soon they will be called in.

"Did you hear that?" Morgenbesser already feels self-conscious about his loss of control. "'A hint of figs in the Chardonnay.' Jesus. 'The wine has great structure. It doesn't promise anything it can't deliver.' What are they talking about? A bottle of wine or a candidate running for office?"

"The public radio wine reviewers?" Amy can't quite fit the annoyance with the outburst.

"Who comes up with this copy? 'A hint of figs.' Give me a break!"

"I was just looking up figs today. Their symbolic significance. Somehow my students got on the subject. It came up in a poem." Amy teaches Comparative Literature at the university. It was through her influence that Morgenbesser got his adjunct faculty appointment. "The fig is a symbol of fecundity, life, prosperity. The fig *leaf* represents lust and sex. Plutarch says it resembles the male sex organ."

"Adam and Eve used it to cover their nakedness." Morgenbesser's comment is almost an afterthought. He's still reeling from the earlier agitation that underlay his explosion, which began with an encounter with Ellen Herxheimer at the athletic club.

"Hence, its use in statuary and painting during the Victorian period when 'modesty' was in vogue."

"I don't give a fig," Morgenbesser muses. "That's not worth a fig. Somebody must have said that in Shakespeare. I can almost hear it. Meaning, 'worthless.' A fig is something with little value."

"The fig itself is the female principle," Amy corrects in her professorial voice. "If the fig leaf is male, linga, the fig itself is female, yoni. A basket of figs is fertility and represents the woman as goddess or mother."

"Okay, well, I wish I'd bought a bottle of Chardonnay instead of the Manischewitz blackberry." He remembers Kim, the pretty blonde girl who sold him the wine, with a pang of wistful desire. A girl half his age.

Amy laughs. "Why don't you go call in the kids? It's time to light candles."

* * *

After work, Morgenbesser stops by the athletic club for a quick workout and shower before stopping at the bakery for a loaf of chollah and the wine store for the Manischewitz. He runs into Ellen Herxheimer on the exercise bikes. He usually does not go to the athletic club on Fridays, but he had to leave work early for an appointment with the optometrist, to get a new prescription for eyeglasses, and seeing as he had some time on his hands, he decided to go for some exercise. He is surprised to find Ellen there, too.

"Good shabbos," he hails her, a kind of mock greeting under the circumstances. She is toiling away on one of the stationary bicycles with a women's magazine in front of her.

"Oh, hi!" Ellen chirps in her sing-song voice, looking up, and then she giggles. "You know, I really don't think of you as Jewish."

"Really." Morgenbesser's response is more like a deflection, a defense. There they are, rooting around his identity again. What he is. What he isn't. A recurring theme in his encounters with Ellen, the psychologist, the social worker.

"No, I have to confess it. When you just said that to me just now? About shabbos? I thought, 'he's talking about my tribe.'"

"Huh, that's interesting." What else is there to say? He climbs onto the bike next to hers, his heart suddenly heavy.

"Do you *feel* Jewish? I know I've asked you a hundred times, but you always reply with all kinds of complexity attached. I just want a simple answer."

"Betwixt and between, I guess."

Ellen smiles—triumphantly, it seems to Morgenbesser. He wants to let the matter drop, and Ellen turns back to her women's magazine, but he has to say something, doesn't he? Yet, not wanting to appear super-serious, he exclaims with the sort of mock urgency that might be taken for sarcasm: "But I *am* a Jew! I *am*! I *am* a Jew! Just the very fact that I have these doubts, Ellen! Doesn't that go for something? If one of the hallmarks of a Jew is being in a constant state of doubt, well, then I'm an ur-Jew! Can't say I'm a Christian, can't say I'm a Jew. Can't even say if Christian is the opposite of Jew. Which all raises the question, what exactly *is* a Jew, anyway? And why can't you 'think' of me as a Jew?" He answers for her, continuing in the sarcastic vein: "Well, your childhood wasn't like mine. You celebrated Christmas. You ate bacon. Your people murdered my people. Hey, besides, it's a genetic thing. Look at me; even if you can't tell by my name, you know I'm a Jew. The nose, the eyes, the facial structure. Even the hair. But you? Jewish? With your looks? Who do you think you're kidding? 'Jew by choice'? Give me a break!"

Ellen laughs at his mimicry. She knows she has the upper hand. Though she looks young for her age, she is still a few years older than Morgenbesser, and there's a subtle erotic give-and-take in their exchanges, a struggle for command. A hint of figs. "I think it's because you don't 'look' Jewish," she decides. "But also because you seem to be a tag-along Jew, as most of us are. But if you flat-out said you felt Jewish, I'd redefine you in my mind as Jewish. You definitely get Jew points for being an active member of your synagogue."

She's trying to placate him now, Morgenbesser thinks. Just when he had her telling him about *him*.

"How many Jew points add up to being a Jew? And what does it mean to 'feel' Jewish, and if you don't 'feel' Jewish does that necessarily mean you 'feel' some other quality that is the same sort of thing as being 'Jewish' only a different flavor? Gentile, say, or Christian or Buddhist or Muslim? I guess I lead a sort of Jewish life if you mean I go to the synagogue regularly with my family, but does that make me Jewish? To be Jewish means to be born of a Jewish mother—that's irrevocable, right? The defining factor. Or can you convert to Christianity, say, and still 'look' Jewish but not *be* a Jew?"

"I have a friend, Phil, who was born Jewish, but he's into some sort of weird Christian beliefs. But no, I don't really think of him as a Jew. I just think he's strange—odd, like all cultists. But just tell me, Daniel. Do you *feel* Jewish?"

"Tell me what that feels 'like' and I'll tell you. I've noticed no discernable differences in the way I've essentially 'felt' since I first came to consciousness. What I feel, though, is older and less attractive, feel my own mortality like a cold breath on my neck. Feel a little hungry, feel a little disoriented. I mean, I feel a little skeptical about feeling much of anything.

"Tag-along Jews. Could that be the very essence of a convert? There are those who convert and go overboard for the lifestyle, the kashruth, the Shabbat restrictions, the punctilious observance, and then there are those who convert for *shalom bayit*, and is that tag-along-ness? 'Tag-along' meaning without any particular convictions? Has that ring to it. Did I mention that I participate in a minyan at work? If by 'participate' we mean being a warm body, counted as Jewish, to help make up ten male Jewish bodies, in a room facing east while the very conscientious types bow and davan and sway. Ten minutes later, they thank me for having joined. Does this make me a Jew?"

"You're a good guy, Daniel; you're a mensch. Everybody's mortal. Everybody's older than they were. You're attractive; you stay fit." She gestures to indicate his current activity on the bike, and Morgenbesser wonders if he sounded as if he were fishing for a compliment or at least for reassurance. He has a sudden curiosity about what sex would be like with Ellen, a powerful inchoate image, the two of them in bed together. "But what do you mean," she says, interrupting his reverie, "by 'coming to consciousness'? I don't get it."

"I was just talking about not feeling essentially any different; there was this ritual when I converted, this ceremony, involving the mikvah and saying certain prayers, but there was no *presto! change-o!* experience. Know what I'm saying? One's perceptions of the world change as one grows older, but the essential 'Daniel Morgenbesser-ness' of my experience seems pretty much a constant from when I first started identifying with it. The who-I-am."

"Just tell me, do you *feel* Jewish?"

"Just tell me, what does that feel *like*?"

"Oh, Daniel. That question's way too big."

"Then how can you ask me if I *feel* Jewish?"

* * *

It's a busy evening at the liquor store when Morgenbesser rolls in after stopping first at the bakery for the loaf of chollah. Friday night. Kim is behind the cash register, ringing up the six packs and the quarts of vodka and scotch. She's a pretty blue-eyed blonde girl in tight jeans, her hair long and loose, an athletic undergraduate air about her, and Morgenbesser's been flirting with her for about a year, since she started working here. It's innocent, playful, based on beer jokes, with a mild sexual undercurrent. A hint of figs. She flirting with an older guy, he flirting with a younger woman.

Morgenbesser puts his purchases on the counter as they greet each other. A bottle of Manischewitz blackberry and a six pack of Samuel Adams.

"Looks like you're in for a big Friday night." Kim rings up the bottles.

"Yeah, nothing like a bottle of Manishewitz wine to slake your thirst."

"Are you Jewish?"

"Yes." A simple answer. Morgenbesser feels confident enough in his answer because of Kim's blondeness, though he does feel compelled to explain about the conversion. Her blondness stops him, though. Why complicate matters?

"Seriously, you're Jewish?"

"Yeah, I really am." He feels a small pang of regret letting the information out; it seems to put a whole new gestalt on the flirtation. How accurate is it, besides? Shouldn't he be qualifying his answer? Explaining? "It's for the Friday night prayers."

"And you can't use any other sort of wine?"

"Well, I guess I could, but it *is* kosher wine, though I guess nobody would notice if I used something else. But I kind of like the sweetness of the Manischewitz, you know? That cough syrupy flavor."

Kim rolls her eyes, and he wonders all at once about her not recognizing him as a Jew since he doesn't fit the general type, an assumption not unlike Ellen's. Is he or isn't he? "Well, have a good night!" Kim's eyes sparkle coyly as she hands him his change.

Morgenbesser steps out of line with his purchases. She's moved on to the next customer, and Morgenbesser leaves wondering what it will be like the next time he comes in for a package of beer.

* * *

As they get ready for bed, Amy comments that he's seemed pretty frazzled this evening. "Anything wrong? Something happen at work?"

"Nah, it was just…I guess I'm just tired."

"Friday nights are such a relief." They continue to undress in silence for a few moments more.

"I ran into Ellen Herxheimer at the athletic club," Morgenbesser finally says.

"Oh yeah? How's she?"

"Okay, I guess. I was sort of surprised to find her there."

"Because of Shabbos? I don't think she's all that observant. I think she belongs to one of those Jewish meditation groups."

"Oh yeah? Kabbalah?"

"Or whatever. Breathing exercises? I don't know."

"She told me she didn't think of me as Jewish."

"Oh yeah?" Amy's voice softens; she begins to comprehend her husband's testiness earlier in the evening.

"We talked about it for a while, what it means to be Jewish."

"What's it mean? According to Ellen."

"Well, we didn't talk about what it meant so much as what it *felt* like."

"What does it *feel* like?" Amy's voice contains a tease, and Morgenbesser looks over at her and all at once realizes that none of that matters. It doesn't matter what Ellen Herxheimer thinks, and it doesn't matter what Kim at the liquor store thinks.

"Here, feel this."

"Well, what have we here?"

Amy touches him intimately, and Morgenbesser draws his wife towards him. Soon he is overwhelmed by figs, by the smell and the taste and the feel of figs.